Uncle Sean

The Early Journals of Will Barnett,

Book 1

by

Ronald L. Donaghe

Two Brothers Press

Copyright © 2004, © 2022
by Ronald L. Donaghe

No part of this book may be reproduced or transmitted in any form or by any means, graphic, electronic, or mechanical, including photocopying, recording, taping, or by any information storage retrieval system, without the express permission in writing from the author. Permission is herein granted for excerpts used in book reviews.

This is a work of fiction. All characters and incidents described are strictly the creation of the author, and any resemblance to real people, living or dead, or real incidents of similar nature is purely coincidental.

A Two Brothers Press Book
ISBN: 9798201401498

The Early Journals of Will Barnett consists of three separate novels:

Uncle Sean, Book 1
Lance, Book 2
All Over Him, Book 3

These three novels were first published in the United States in Trade Paper in 2004.

This Two Brothers Press revised Edition (2022) is printed and distributed by arrangement with Draft2Digital.com.

Spanish language editions, *Tío Sean, Lance,* and *Todo Sobre El* were first published in Barcelona, Spain, in 2005. © Editorial EGALES, S.I. 2005, Cervantes, 2. 08002 Barcelona: www.editorialegales.com

Cover design by Ronald L. Donaghe on these 2022 editions of the three-book series.

Painting by Henry Scott Tuke - The Bridgeman Art Library, Object 361444, Public Domain:
https://commons.wikimedia.org/w/index.php?curid=23215075

Dedication

This book is lovingly dedicated to all young gay people who have lived in isolation in time and place, who have had to discover by themselves those sweet and painful feelings of attraction for members of the same sex. Be not afraid. Others have come before you and others will come after.

Uncle Sean
From the Journals of Will Barnett

A Novel

Ronald L. Donaghe

Contents

PART ONE THE *BIG CHIEF* TABLET 9

    ONE IN THE SHADOW OF VIETNAM 13

    TWO BETRAYED TRUST 38

    THREE AWAKENING 50

    FOUR DISAPPOINTMENT AND A LESSON 57

    FIVE MIDNIGHT COWBOY & THE TWO MEN 66

    SIX HALCYON MOMENTS... 82

PART TWO THE LETTER 87

PART THREE THE SPIRAL NOTEBOOK 97

    ONE DISCOVERY 97

    TWO GROWTH 106

    THREE AWAKENED TO MATURITY 113

    FOUR BEGINNING TO UNDERSTAND AND HOPE 116

    FIVE HOW THINGS CHANGE 119

    SIX THE KID ON THE BLUFF 123

    SEVEN STRUCK DUMB 137

    EIGHT HIS NAME IS LANCE 148

    NINE NERVOUS & STRANGE 152

    TEN HOPES AND PLANS—AWRY 164

    ELEVEN THE PASSING 186

    TWELVE HINTS OF A NEW LIFE 192

Part One
The Big Chief Tablet

The way certain materials came into my possession (including a *Big Chief* tablet, a letter, dog tags from the Vietnam Era, and a spiral notebook) is somewhat startling. Had it not been so hellishly hot, when I was tearing down the old barn, however, I might never have stopped the demolition long enough to notice the box that tumbled out of the rafters and fell onto the heap of trash I was going to haul off. As it was, though, we stopped frequently to rest and drink beer to reconstitute our body fluids, and it was during one of these rest periods when the box came into my possession.

I was tearing down the old barn twenty miles south of Hachita, New Mexico, just west of the Big Hatchet mountains, where a long-time-ago farm had passed into oblivion. One of the nearby ranchers by the name of Hill had asked me to perform this demolition. I wasn't being paid for the work, but from experience, I knew what old lumber from the turn of the century could be worth. Very little remained of the other farm buildings, but it was as if the barn had held the small treasure of documents through the years, and gave them up only when they were in danger of being lost forever.

I had already removed the roofing tin and the sub-roof of one-by-eights, laying them aside for salvage, as they were remarkably well preserved. Because of the dry climate of Southwestern New Mexico, salvaging materials from old buildings is often rewarding. Yet, the very forces of dry weather and hot sun that can preserve material can also destroy it. I had already torn off much of the siding, which was not in such good shape; it was a form of fiber-board that had long since warped under the relentless sun, falling to pieces under the crowbars, hammers, and other implements I often use in this work.

So it was that, when the barn was merely a skeleton of itself, I was standing inside the slatted shadows cast by the remaining rafters, when the box fell the nearly thirty feet to the pile of rubbish in the middle of the floor. Sealed with disintegrating duct tape, it simply burst open upon impact. Although there was evidence of some ruin due to mice and insects, when I kneeled over the contents that had spilled out, I was amazed at the condition of the *Big Chief* tablet. I chose to pick it up first, since I had not seen one for at least thirty years. As I turned the pages, I saw that the entire tablet was filled with what looked like a young person's handwriting (due to the formation of the letters as much as anything else) with very little space left for margins, in a small script that was difficult to read, considering the way the ink had spread into the fibers of the pulpy paper.

Realizing almost immediately that it was a diary or journal of some sort, and being a writer, myself, I treated this tablet and the other two documents with utmost care. After having read only part way into the contents of the tablet, I realized its value. The letter was written in an obviously more mature hand — and not that of the young writer. It was on regular typing paper from an era long gone, in that it was thicker than modern typing paper, only slightly yellowed after what must be twenty or thirty years. The salutation was simply to Will, and was signed simply as Sean. Yet I knew that it must have been special to whoever Will was, because it was much creased and tri-folded; perhaps even carried around in a pants' hip pocket before being placed in the box. Who knew? The spiral notebook, like the *Big Chief* tablet, was much used. As I flipped through the pages, I saw that sometimes the writing was controlled and neatly written; at other times, it was scrawled, as if written in a hurry or when the author was sitting in an awkward position (maybe). While the writing in the spiral notebook appeared to be authored by the same hand as that in the *Big Chief* tablet, it was markedly improved in both expression and control of the cursive, itself. The most curious item in this collection, of course, was the set of dog tags that bore the name Sean Martin; who he was and how his tags came to be among the collection of writings would have to be revealed by the writing itself. Of themselves, the tags revealed only that the writer of the letter was Sean Martin, that he had been registered in the Army during the Vietnam era, and that the presence of the dog tags in the box was important to Will. But I could tell no more than that without further examination.

I was so excited by the find that I took the afternoon off, sent my crew home, and sat in Kranberry's Restaurant in nearby Lordsburg for much of the afternoon and into the dinner hour reading from beginning to end from the *Big Chief* tablet, to the letter, and to the very last page in the spiral notebook. I found myself subconsciously thumbing the raised lettering of the dog tags as I read and only noticed that I was doing so when the waitress interrupted me to pour more coffee, or when I reluctantly got up to use the Men's Room. Taken all together, the tablet, the letter, and the spiral notebook made up an amazing story. But I will let the documents speak for themselves. While I have taken some liberties with the material (inserting clarifying marks of punctuation, puzzling out ruined or smudged portions of the writing by the context of the surrounding material, and ferreting out more sensible sentences and paragraphs), I have not interfered with the "voice" in any of the materials. I've also broken down the writing into "chapters" to aid readers in approximate breaks in time, though some other person editing this material might have chosen to divide the material differently.

<>

One
In the Shadow of Vietnam

Uncle Sean sure is pretty. But there's something wrong with him, anyway. I got to write about this though. My chest feels all funny, and I don't think he knows I've been looking at him, least not so he really notices much. I'm only fourteen though Mama says I'm big for my age.

    I know I don't write good. Daddy don't believe too much in book learnin', so I got the old Webster's down from the shelf, so I can look up words. Come to think of it, I don't know as I'll be letting nobody read it. But I got to write here in this tablet.

    When I went into town with Daddy in the pickup, I got me this *Big Chief* tablet. We was picking up some fertilizer for the cotton, and since it's so hot the end of May, we went into the Rexall and he bought us sodas, and I seen the school supplies and got this idea I wanted to write down how Uncle Sean is so pretty and how it makes me feel. So, I asked Daddy if I could buy me the tablet and one of them blue pens for 19 cents.

I told him I like to draw and he says "you ain't no sissy," and I said I ain't and I told him, "when I go back to school in the fall, I want to draw hotrods since people like to race on the flats up near Lordsburg and drawing pictures is fun."

He acted like it was too much bother, but when he was finishing up his soda, he slaps a dollar on the table, then grins and says "well, what you waitin' on?"

I kept the *Big Chief* and the pen in the sack they give me at the Rexall and, on the way home, I held it in my lap and tried to pretend it weren't much, me buying it and all, but Daddy, he keeps looking over at me and shaking his head.

"I ain't never seen much use in book learnin'," he says. "If you ain't got a strong back and hard hands, you ain't gonna make it. But I reckon other boys'll draw them hotrods, too."

But I do have a strong back and all. So, even though there's smudges now from what I wrote down, cause I got grease on my hands from helping Daddy with the equipment, I got to write, and ain't got much time to wash the grease off with gasoline before I can sneak off.

The sun's nearly down and I've snuck into the barn, up in the loft. I don't think nobody saw me though and I got the Webster's tucked up under the rafters. Nobody's gonna miss it, least not right away.

It's hot up here, though, so I shucked my shirt. And I can see way out from up here, looking east toward the Big Hatchet Mountain. It's still light enough to see, too, and I got good eyes. Long as I get my chores done before supper nobody comes looking for me, neither.

So, Uncle Sean. He came back from Vietnam Christmas of '68. That was last winter. Mama says he's lucky he weren't killed, but there's *something* wrong with him. He's real mad and quiet, and he and Daddy yell at each other, and Daddy says if he weren't Mama's brother, he'd fire him. But you can't fire kin.

I come in to the kitchen that morning, the day after Christmas, and there he was sitting at the table with Mama and Daddy, drinking coffee. And Mama says, "Will, come here and say hi to your Uncle Sean. You ain't seen him since you was about six, so you probably don't remember him."

And I didn't and he looks up at me and I'm staring into his eyes the color of cornflowers, a blue so pale they swam. The way the light struck his face from the sun coming in through the kitchen window over the sink put a glow over his blond hair, too, and though he's got darkish brown eyebrows, they're real pretty shaped and his eye lashes are black and kind of wet looking. He smiled at me, and I must have stood there slack jawed like a dimwit. I never seen such soft girlish lips on a guy before. Now, he don't put on none of Mama's Revlon or nothing but they're pink and soft anyway.

My hands are shaking so much but I'm gonna write this: I wondered right then how it'd feel to kiss those lips. I get a sweet feeling sometimes just wondering about that.

I never felt much a couple a years ago about things like this in the way I feel funny in my chest, now, every time I get a close look at him. His blue eyes cut right through me when he gives me one of his funny, straight-on looks and kind of grins when he don't think Daddy's looking. Like it's me and him in on some kind of joke on Daddy. Specially when Daddy's all hot and sweaty and him and Uncle Sean have been yelling. But I guess that comes later, cause I'm writing about the first time I laid eyes on him, and how it was like a crush or something. I know about crushes because my two oldest sisters, Julianne and Marsha, used to get them all the time.

Now that it's hot, he don't wear no shirt, neither. And they fed him good in the army and made him do pushups and tote stuff when they was on patrol, though he don't talk about that, except to tell me I don't want none of it, so stay on the farm and get what he calls a deferment or something like that.

I tell him "What am I gonna do but stay right here?" because Mama and Daddy just had me and my five sisters, Julianne, Marsha, May, Rita, and Trinket—two of them are younger than me, and three of them are older. Julianne and Marsha got out as soon as they graduated high school and never looked back. But even though May is older than me, it's not by much, and we're actually the closest.

So, Uncle Sean's chest is all nice and muscled, and his arms are ropy with muscles. Mine are too, because of my size, and I been working along side Daddy since I was like six years old.

Then he wears them fatigues. He says "why throw away good work clothes?" They hang low on his waist and I can tell he don't wear nothing underneath. I sometimes see the wiry hair on his patch, though mine ain't nothing much yet.

So, Christmas. I sat right down and started in talking to him and he's polite and quiet, and Mama says, "don't pester him, he drove all night." Then I got to help him bring his stuff in from the car. He got Julianne and Marsha's room right off the bathroom, and he didn't have much stuff.

I asked him, "why don't you have one of them rifles from the army? I thought they let you keep stuff like that, or at least a dagger, or some kind of neat knife." But he looked funny when I said that, but he still smiled and said, "because I don't want anything that can kill. I've had enough of that."

So, I knew enough to clam up about it, hoping he weren't mad at me for talking about rifles and daggers. But he did have a duffel bag, a bunch a boots, and boxes with some books. And he pulled things out and I asked him if he minded if I watched him and he said, "no, but don't touch anything unless I give it to you." But I didn't care about touching none of his stuff. So I sat on the bed and watched him, the way his back looked once he'd shucked his jacket and the way his hair hung down over the neck of his t-shirt, kind of curled at the ends cause he needed a haircut, and the way his hands looked kind of slim and smooth when he took stuff out of his duffel bag and shook out shirts and pants and things.

He put a picture out on the dresser. It was a picture with two guys in it, arms around each other's shoulders. I went over to it and he says, "you can pick it up," so first thing I did was see right off it was him, looking real pretty like I say, smiling real big, and so was the other guy, and it made me feel all funny looking at it, and I wanted to keep it. I asked him "who's that?" and he looked, and I watched his eyes and they turned all sad, and then he took the picture from me and said to run along. He needs to get some sleep. He drove all night.

Mama was doing dishes, and my two little sisters were eating cereal. Daddy and May were outside, though there wasn't much to do, as it was cold and the wind had already picked up. So, I dried dishes and asked Mama where Uncle Sean come from that he drove all night and she says San Antonio, Texas.

"But I thought he was in the army," I said.

"He was," she said, "but he's been in the hospital," and I asked what for, and she looked out the kitchen window then looked back at me.

"You go on, now, Will. When Sean gets up you can show him around."

So, I went outside, and Daddy and May were on the sunny side of the barn sitting in between the big doors where the wind wasn't whistling past. It faces east, but where they were, you can see south and the mountains all the way down into Mexico from there. They had drug a tarp out of the barn and laid it open and were working on a transmission from the cotton picker. May's older than me by just eleven months, makin' her fifteen, right now, and me and her are the only ones that like to work outside, even though Mama makes everybody work outside some of the time. Me and May, though, do it because we want to. So when I ain't in the mood to help Daddy, May usually is, and when May ain't, I am. So, we're kind'a good buddies, besides being brother and sister, though we don't look nothin' alike, as I got blond hair and blue eyes and May's got red hair and green eyes, and freckles, and turns red from her teeth to her toenails when it's hot out. I tan pretty good.

Daddy's older than Mama, and he's got black hair and dark brown eyes and thin lips and strong arms and big hands with black hair on the back of them. So, when I found May and Daddy working together, both with grease on their hands, I thought about Uncle Sean and how pretty he was as I watched Daddy work and May handing him tools out of the toolbox.

"Mama says Uncle Sean's been in the hospital," I said. "Was he wounded?" May squints up at me, and Daddy didn't look up at me, just kept working. But he stopped for a second, hunching his shoulders like he was about to lift something heavy.

"No, he weren't wounded," he said. "Now you gonna talk or help me?"

So, anyway, there's something wrong with Uncle Sean. Cause I saw that sad look that December morning and I knew not to ask too many questions, since both Mama and Daddy acted like they didn't want to talk about it, neither.

So later, when Uncle Sean got up and we all ate lunch, Mama says "you take Uncle Sean and show him around." Daddy gave me the keys to the pickup and said, "show Sean how well you can drive," and Uncle Sean grinned at me with those pretty lips and says "you won't run off the road will you?"

I felt as goosey as a girl. Don't ask me why, but I seen the way Julianne and Marsha acted when their boyfriends would drive up and they would squeak and giggle, and so I felt like that, only I didn't show nothing as I drove.

Our farm is cut up into different sections, cause of the arroyos running through the property, and we farm one patch here and one patch there. "Me and Daddy built this bridge," I say, as we drive over it. Most of our farm lies north of the house, but I headed out south, first from the barn, down the Hill place road. It's a ranch on the south of us. When we turned west about a mile from the house, we came to the bridge.

"We built it out of railroad ties," I tell him. "Got them from the old rail line that ran past here when they was shipping out the ore from those hills yonder."

And Uncle Sean looked out the window as we passed over the bridge. Then, when we were on the westward road, we both looked around at the bare ground. He sighed. His left arm was on the back of the seat and he dropped his hand down onto my shoulder. I giggled a little, cause when he squeezed my shoulder I felt a twinge down in my pants.

"It looks the same as when I was a kid," he said. "You were too little to remember, but I'd stay for the summers with your daddy and Arlene" (Uncle Sean meant my mama).

"Except it was greener. Right? In the summer?"

"Just where the crops grow," he said. "But the desert looks just the same."

I had my window down with cold air blowing through, and Uncle Sean rolled his window down. He was wearing a camouflage jacket I bet he got from the army, and a ugly, green T-shirt. All I had on was a T-shirt and my Levi jacket, but I wasn't cold at all the way he squeezed my shoulder. It was most unconscious I think, cause he squeezed and looked out the windows, and I glanced at his face and sighed, quiet like, cause even from the side his lips were that pretty pink and his lashes seemed to droop, like he was sad.

"Why were you in the hospital?" I asked, before I knew I was going to, but he didn't answer, like he didn't hear me.

Then later, I asked him why, out of the whole wide world, he'd come back here. "Nobody stays," I tell him, "Except maybe boys like me who got to take over the land when our dads die."

We been all over the farm by now, a whole lot of nothing to see and we're pulling into the drive next to the barn.

"I came back here," he says, looking over at me, his lashes so long they're touching his cheeks, and his pink lips are kind of wet like, cause he's been running his tongue over them. "Because I don't have any place else in the world to go. At least not right now."

"I'm glad you're here, Uncle Sean," I say. I want to say, *because I love you*, but I don't. I'm kind of afraid of him, he's so pretty.

***

Mama came from a big family. She's the oldest of six children. Uncle Sean is the youngest, near twenty-two. Mama says he was drafted into the army straight out of high school, from down south, near Louisiana. That's where they're from. Shreveport or some place. I was asking her about her kin because I was wondering why Uncle Sean says he ain't got no place else to go.

She was making fried pies out of some peaches she put up in Mason jars she said she needed to use up. Uncle Sean and Daddy had went over to Luna County for some parts and Rita, May, and Trinket (that's what we call my littlest sister, Shawna, because she's so little even though she's eight) went over to a birthday party and a sleep over at Julie Collins' this afternoon. And Mama made me help her with the pies. The best ones are the fried pies dipped in powdered sugar, and we were eating one a piece, and I asked her why Uncle Sean says he ain't got no place else to go.

She's smoking a cigarette and has flour on the side of her hand, where she smoothed out the flour on the rolling board for the crust. Mama's pretty too, so I see where Uncle Sean gets it. Only Mama's old. At least forty-five, and her forehead's got deep worry lines. And she's got green eyes, not blue like Uncle Sean.

"Well your granny and grandpa Martin are dead," Mama says, "and Sean's the baby of the family. Your aunts and uncles are married and have kids and don't have room. Besides, Sean used to come stay with me when he was about your age. He always came out from Louisiana in the summers, and it just seemed natural, once he was discharged that he'd come here."

"How come he ain't married?" I asked Mama, and she got this funny look and wiped a strand of hair away from her face and got flour on her cheek.

"Lord, give him time!" She says. "Honey, that war ain't no good on those young boys they send over there. Sean was only nineteen and he was over there almost two years, before they sent him home to be laid up in a hospital."

"Was he shot or not?!" I say, then, because nobody will tell me. "How can you be in the hospital so long if you ain't wounded!" I kind of raised my voice at that. "He don't seem wounded," I say. "He don't limp or anything."

She takes a deep drag off her cigarette, which is almost smoked to the filter. "I reckon you're gonna pester me till I tell you," she says, smashing out the butt in an ashtray on the table. Then she says, "He had a nervous breakdown, honey, but don't you go tellin' him I said so."

I asked her what that was, but she wouldn't tell me. "You just don't say a word about that to your uncle, hear me?"

***

So, there's something wrong with Uncle Sean and it makes me sad. We had a school bus driver once that had a nervous breakdown, least that's what people said. But I think she just up and quit because some of the high school boys were mean to her. One day they opened the emergency doors in the back of the bus, as we were rolling down the road, and shoved the spare tire out, and all of us got up and went to the back watching it hit the gravel and bounce off like a ball, and Mrs. Mack hits the brakes and goes into a skid on the gravel road, and we come to a stop half on the road and half into a shallow arroyo. It was a couple a hours before old man Hill comes along. Mrs. Mack screamed herself raw at us, even though it was only a couple of the mean guys that did it. And then we was there another couple a hours before Mr. Hill gets back with a tractor to pull the bus out of the arroyo. Next day we had a new driver. Dosier *Duffus* is what we called him, cause he was big and hefty, but had a tiny brain, only he could slap even the biggest high school guy around with one hand, and he says, "you give Mrs. Mack a nervous breakdown."

So, I figured people in the army was mean to Uncle Sean.

Well. That's about it for when Uncle Sean got here at Christmas. I was real happy he was here. But I was kind of bothered, like would he like me? Was he crazy? And well...I don't know how to say what it makes me feel like with him here.

***

Uncle Sean says Americans don't know what's going on there in Vietnam, says we're killing women and children. That's all he says before he gets quiet. But that's not what's wrong with him. Things like that'd bother anybody.

At supper one night, Daddy was talking about the war, and says how weak-minded them boys over in Vietnam are, cause they're all hopped up on that devil's weed like damn fools and when he was in the army in world war number two, men was men, and didn't need no drugs and Uncle Sean was real quiet. This time, though, when he looked over at me with those eyes, they didn't have that jokey kind of thing we share. Instead, it was kind of like he was about to cry and his Revlon pink lips were pressed tight together.

And I knew he was sad about something or mad at Daddy for talking like a damn fool, knowing Uncle Sean was in the hospital with a nervous breakdown, and that night that funny feeling got so sweet in my chest when Uncle Sean looked over at me and I saw the tears, I just said, "Daddy, shut up! You ain't been over there. Uncle Sean ain't no damn fool even if he was in the army."

I got slapped good for that, and Daddy finished eating in silence, only he looked mad and clamped his jaws shut, and Mama sent the girls off to the kitchen to start on the dishes. So, it was just me and Mama and Daddy and Uncle Sean at the table, and

Mama says, "Roy (my daddy), Will's right. You ain't been over there. It's a different kind of war and you know it."

And Daddy says he knew it so everybody just think what they want. It's his house and his farm and he'll speak his mind if he's a mind to.

I felt sorry for Daddy, too, right then, even though my face felt all hot where he'd slapped me. But Daddy held back. I could tell. I give him that. He don't hit us like I saw him hit old Bob Hill one day, right in the face with his fist over some cow that had got into the corn and trampled it to the ground.

Then Uncle Sean says real quiet, head bowed, looking at Daddy, then sneaking a look at me, cause he knows I stood up for him, "you're right, Roy. No hard feelings, here. Will didn't mean to be disrespectful." Then he turns to me and my chest is heaving, and I know tears are in my eyes, too, and he says, "Will, you're too young to tell your daddy to shut up, but I know you thought Roy was after me."

But sometimes I know Daddy gets onto Uncle Sean for no reason, cause he's mad about him being here since Christmas.

So, everybody calmed down and later on, when Mama, Daddy, and May were watching television, and Rita and Trinket were put to bed, Uncle Sean left the house. He's got a car, a real neat '57 Chevy, but he don't go nowhere much. Too far over to Luna County, and right now he says he ain't got no money. So, I saw him through the screen door in the kitchen head out to his car. Heard him slam the door shut, and I listened for the kick of the engine, but it stayed quiet. So later, I snuck out through the back door and came up behind the car, where I could see the back of Uncle Sean's head behind the wheel, just sitting there, smoke curling out of the window on his side giving off a funny kind of smell, not like what Mama smokes.

He didn't have the radio blaring, neither, because out here about the only station you can pick up is KOMA out of Oklahoma City. And like as not it comes and goes. So I figured if he looked into his rear-view mirror he could see me even if it was kind of dark out, though it don't really get dark 'til around nine or so.

So, I make out like I'm just walking past the car heading out to the barn. As I pass by, I say, "Hi, Uncle Sean. What kind a smokes you got? They smell like burning tumbleweeds."

Funny, even though it's near dark, his paler-than-blue eyes catch mine and hold me. He's got his elbow out the window.

"Roll my own," he says, and kind of talks like he's trying to suck his breath back in. I don't smoke but I say, "let me try one." He says "no, but come here." Then I stand right up next to the car, and he's not wearing a shirt and I can see sweat glistening off his chest and shining on his neck. He shows me the smoke.

"I'm going to give you a 'shotgun,' though," he says, grinning at me. "Get ready to suck in the smoke." Then he purses his lips. "Do like that." So, I make a small "o" with my mouth and he sticks the burning end of his home-rolled in his mouth and pulls my face down to his lips. I let him pull my face to his, and just when I'm all ready to kiss him, because that's what I think he wants, he blows smoke out and I breathe it in.

I try to pull away because it's near making me cough but he keeps my lips near his and keeps blowing smoke and I keep sucking it in.

"Now hold it!" he says, taking the cigarette out of his mouth.

A minute later, I felt like I was getting dizzy, and he's still holding my face close to his, and I get that goosey twinge in my pants, feeling how hot his hand is on the back of my neck and his breath is right in my face. And even up close in the dark, like this, his face is all smooth and pretty.

"Get in," he says, and I go around and open the passenger side and get in. His whole car smells like burning tumbleweeds.

So, we're sitting in the car and it's still like ninety degrees out and I'm sweating and think it would be nice in the house at least with the swamp cooler running, but I wouldn't trade places for nothing. And he says, "you don't need to stand up for me like you did in there." He cocks his head toward the house. "Your dad's not a bad man, Will."

"Then how come you two fight all the time?" I say.

He chuckles down in his throat, looking over at me in the dark, and where I'm sitting, I see the porch light reflecting in his eyes and they're shiny with tears and I feel sorry for him.

He says, "I don't know, Will. Maybe he doesn't like me being here. I'd leave if I could."

"I don't want you to go, Uncle Sean!" I say. "You said you don't have nowhere else in the whole wide world to go, and Mama says so, too."

"Arlene's been talking to you about me?" Uncle Sean says. "Does she want me to go, too?"

"No! Uncle Sean, she says you can't go, cause all your other sisters and brothers are too busy, and since you been in the hospital—"

I shut up quick, cause I was about to spill the beans about his nervous breakdown and Mama told me not to say so.

He turns and looks at me, and it's like no matter how dark, his face can find the light, cause I see real clear how sad he looks. My chest feels so funny, looking at him. I wisht he'd of kissed me a minute ago, instead of blow smoke in my face.

"Did she tell you why I was in the hospital, Will?" His voice is so soft and gentle, I don't know if it's really a question for me, but maybe for him, like he maybe don't know.

"Mama says you had some kind a breakdown. Was people mean to you, Uncle Sean, down there in Vietnam?"

He's still looking at me and smiles. I can feel the heat from his body even though I'm sweating. "It is a country at war with itself," he says. "People are mean to each other when that happens."

"Then how come you were in the hospital?" I asked, but I'm afraid he'll be mad at me for asking again, cause last time he didn't tell me.

Uncle Sean don't pay me no mind, just then, like maybe he hears things in his head too loud to hear me. I think he's angry a lot and I know from how he puts things that it ain't Daddy he's mad at.

Then Uncle Sean looks away, and I watch his chest rise and fall, like he's taking a deep sigh, and I still feel funny in the chest on top of dizzy in my whole body from taking in that "shotgun" thing he did with his home-rolled. But I don't think it has anything to do with the warm feelings I have for Uncle Sean. I hear him breathing, I watch his chest rise and fall, and watch a drip of sweat run down his neck. It's all different colors, like a tiny glass bead reflecting light.

We sit for awhile longer, quiet, and I can hear the crickets start up in the dark. They're real loud, like they suddenly got real big. Out near the barn, I hear an owl hoot hoot, like I'm Superman with super hearing. And I keep watching Uncle Sean's face and want to move up next to him, put my arm around his shoulder or something, he's so sad.

***

Weren't long after Daddy said those mean things at dinner that him and Uncle Sean had a big fight, and Uncle Sean packed up his car, and just about to drive off, when Mama comes out and says no he's got to stay. Roy didn't mean it. I was off in the field and when I came back the fight was over, but I seen Uncle Sean standing next to his car, and I knew right away that he was mad.

This time, I seen Uncle Sean a different kind of mad than I ever seen. He weren't crying no tears, and he didn't look sad, neither. Mama was, though. She was crying a lot, and I never seen her like that, cause Mama and Daddy, they don't fight much except to raise their voices ever once in a while.

I was really a kid, this time, cause nobody even paid me the least mind. Even Uncle Sean never even glanced at me when I pulled up and seen that Mama was crying, bawling really, hanging onto one of Uncle Sean's hands, and he was standing all straight, looking right past Mama like a pointer dog, back at the house. So I looked over there, but there weren't nothing on the porch.

So real quiet like I went to the house, cause no one paid me no mind and I saw that Daddy was in the kitchen, looking out the window. I seen from the way he was hunched over that he was mad too. But I knew I better not get caught looking at him, so I went down the hall to Uncle Sean's room and, sure enough. it was clean as a whistle.

Then I went to the girls' room and they was all in there looking scared, and so I asked May what happened. And this is what she said.

It seems like Daddy got some strange notion to go into Uncle Sean's room when Uncle Sean was outside. It being June, it really is hot, and maybe Daddy was in there fiddling with the cooler vents or something is all May can figure out. Then he comes out of there, May says, with that picture Uncle Sean has on his dresser, and May and the girls and Mama's in the kitchen making cookies.

But Daddy says he's going to have a talk with Sean, about what's the meaning of that picture. He don't like it, May says, though she don't know why.

Then, when Uncle Sean comes in to wash up, Daddy sends the girls out of the room, but they can hear Daddy start to yell, and May sneaks out in the hall and stands in the living room door, so she can see into the kitchen and Daddy's shaking the picture in Uncle Sean's face.

So, I asked her what he was saying, and when she told me that Daddy was saying they looked like faggots, I got this horrible stomped on feeling down in my guts, cause when guys at school say that, they mean something terrible, though I never knew exactly what, cause the Webster's only says it's firewood. And when I ask May what that means, she looks at me funny and says, "You don't know?" And I say, no, and then she just looks like a imp with her freckles and green eyes and says, "you'll figure it out," but I'm not sure I want to know.

And May says that Uncle Sean stands right up to Daddy, saying how Daddy can put any thought on it he wants but it's his room and to stay the hell out and mind his own business, and Daddy says no it ain't it's his house and if Uncle Sean don't want to live under his rules then to get out.

By the time I left the girls' room, I was angry, like Uncle Sean, cause it weren't fair what Daddy said.

So, anyway, Uncle Sean didn't leave, but everybody was hurt and mad and quiet. It took Daddy a couple a days to tell Uncle Sean that maybe that picture didn't mean what he thought it did. And that was about as close to apologizing as Daddy got.

Now I don't know how Mama got Uncle Sean to stay, cause he was all packed up, but he didn't leave and I let out a big breath about that. But the night of the fight, Uncle Sean stayed in his room and didn't come out for supper, and Mama and Daddy being so old didn't think it was none of us kids' business, like when you ask them questions where they're going and if they don't want you to know they just say to see a man about a dog.

For almost a week, I just wrote; it took everybody awhile to calm down and for us to get back to normal, but I don't think it'll ever be the same, cause for a few days, Daddy sends Uncle Sean off by hisself to work, and keeps me around the barn to help him.

And Daddy fished with questions I could see right through, like what do Uncle Sean and I talk about when we're off by ourselves, and I tell him the truth that Uncle Sean says we ain't going to win that war over in Vietnam, and that we're killing women and children.

Only I know what Daddy was really fishing for, cause him saying that picture of Uncle Sean and his buddy looked like faggots, he was trying to find out if Uncle Sean was doing things to me. At least I got that much out of what faggots are, just like that word, queer, I hear sometimes.

***

One day, Uncle Sean says he's gonna go up to Lordsburg. It's about 40 miles northwest of here, where I got this tablet. I wanted to go with him, cause there wasn't nothing doing in the fields, except irrigating. Him and me got up at four that morning to set the water. But he says he's sorry, but he's got to go fill out some papers and I'd just be bored. Then Mama and the girls say they're gonna go on over to Deming and do some shopping, and that's about 50 miles northeast of here, and so it's me and Daddy and he says he don't need no help. So I'm in the house by myself.

I didn't mean to, but I got this idea. If I put everything back the way I find it, Uncle Sean won't know I been in his room. I been in there a couple of times when he lets me come in. But I don't like to bother him. He likes to read or something, but sometimes after supper, I knock on his door and come in and sit on the edge of his bed and ask him stuff, like how come he ain't married, and who's the guy in the picture on his dresser. But he don't like to answer, especially after what Daddy said, so I think he's hiding something. Maybe what makes him mad and quiet.

So, for awhile after everybody was gone, I just watched television, listening until the house was real quiet. And then I went in his room. I could feel my heart thumping like a John Deere tractor, but I saw Daddy go outside, and from the bedroom window, which ain't got no curtains, any more, I can see from there to the barn and see where Daddy went.

The room is a lot emptier than when my sisters were there. They slept in a double bed, and it's still got the same spread on it, the pink one with the yellow flowers. But the walls are bare, except the outline of where posters of James Dean hung over the bed, and nails where they hung their other pictures. There's a bureau with drawers where Uncle Sean keeps his t-shirts and under shorts and socks, and the top drawer is full of stuff like keys and his dog tags that he kept for some reason. I would've thrown mine away. There's a dresser, too, but the drawers are mostly empty, except for paper and envelopes and stuff and even some sewing stuff Mama keeps in there.

Uncle Sean don't have too many clothes hanging up in the closet, and some of his dirty clothes is laying on the floor of the closet. But there's a box I seen the first day I helped him unpack that's stuck high up on a shelf. So, I pulled up a chair from next to the bed and pulled the box down.

I don't mean to be a snoop, but I got to find out what's wrong with him, cause everybody that knows has clammed up. But what Daddy said got me wondering.

I set it on the floor outside the closet and see how the flaps are folded, so I can fold them back just like they was. It's funny how books smell when they been stored, but these were really strong with that musty odor, like they'd been wet on or something. I think how smart he must be, cause most of the books don't even have pictures, and I flip through the pages and smell the musty dust. One of 'em is a hard back with pages like in a notebook, and it's written in. Pages and pages of lists of things I can hardly read, and each page has a date, like 1967, Saigon, which I never heard of. I was about to put it up when a picture fell out. One of them instant pictures from one of them Kodak cameras that spit out the picture a minute after you take it.

It was kind of faded, but I could tell it was a naked man, wearing something tied around his head and smiling, and holding one of them home-rolled cigarettes. And I can see that it was hot when the picture was taken, because the man is sweating, and his skin is all shiny with it. I flipped it over and it said, "to my man. T.S." I grinned a little that Uncle Sean had a picture of a real naked man not just from the *National Geographic* like I seen. It's kind of hard for me to breathe, too, seeing how pretty T.S. is. So, I get real jumpy and sweat pops out on my face, cause I didn't see right where the picture came out of the book.

So, I just stuck it in the middle of the book, and almost set the book back down in the box when something shiny caught my eye underneath a big envelope in the bottom of the box, and I pulled the envelope up and saw this tin box with all kind of squiggly lines and dragons etched into it. So, I opened it and found more dog tags. Only these weren't Uncle Sean's, and they're bent funny, like something hit along one edge, like if I was to take a hammer and a nail and tried to knock a hole in the metal, and like I was to miss and just graze the edge. And they're all dirty like, with rust spots that flake off, and the chain is broken.

But something in my belly said something was wrong, so I felt the raised words and turned the tags to the light, where I could read the name above a bunch of numbers. It said Theodore Seabrook.

I knew something. It was like I could shut my eyes and hear every tiny sound in the room, the way the beads on the chain on the tags settled back into the tin. I felt funny about the way the rust kind of fell off, too, and flaked on the envelope, which I blew off. I could hear the way the paper rustled when I settled the envelope back down over the tin box. I could even hear my heart pumping my blood as I set the books back in the box.

I knew something that must've made Uncle Sean sad, cause I just bet he pulled those tags off his buddy there in Vietnam, and you wouldn't do that less he was dead.

I felt real guilty like, as I put everything back and moved the chair back to where it was, and then I sat down on the edge of Uncle Sean's bed and took that picture off the dresser. It was him and his buddy, T.S., and in the picture they're both wearing their dog tags. And I hugged it. I couldn't help it.

Two
Betrayed Trust

Ever since I seen that picture in the box and found them dog tags of Theodore Seabrook I knew something about Uncle Sean. Though it's like seeing something and not knowing what to call it. So, then I get this idea.

The layout of our house is like this. The living room and kitchen are on the east side, and everybody comes in the kitchen door, cause that's where the driveway stops. Then off the living room is a hall that runs right down the middle of the house with the bathroom at one end. And Uncle Sean's bedroom is off the hall right near the bathroom, and the window in his room looks south. Then Mama and Daddy's bedroom is up the hall from that, and their window looks west. Then the girl's room is next to Mama and Daddy's, and mine is on the other end of the hall, and I have two windows. One looks north and one looks west. I have the best room in the house when it's hot, because I get cross breezes. And it's really good for sneaking out at night, because I can crawl out the north window, and nobody hears me.

And that's what I did one night, cause I had this idea. It was so hot, everybody had their windows open and were probably laying in bed with no covers on and sweating like pigs. So, I climbed out the window and it was a dark night with no moon and no breeze. I walked barefoot, quick as you please all the way around the house, knowing right where the hydrants were so I wouldn't stub my toe, and when I came around to the south side, I sidled up next to the house, my heart pounding, and I could hardly breathe. I almost changed my mind because I seen that Uncle Sean's window was throwing a square of light into the yard.

It had to of been past midnight, though, cause Mama and Daddy watch Johnnie Carson, and I waited a long time after they shut off the television before I got up. So, I figured either Uncle Sean sleeps with the light burning cause there's something wrong with him and he don't like the dark, or he's maybe reading. So, I took a long, deep breath and let it out real slow. I already had a boner, cause you're not supposed to be a Peeping Tom, and that's just what I was.

I inched my way along the wall, and when I got right up to Uncle Sean's window, I just pulled my head away from the wall and could see into his room, right onto the bed. But he weren't reading. He was laying there holding that picture of him and his buddy, his head was propped up on the pillow, and one arm was under his head. I could see the side of his face, too. I was only about three feet away.

He looked so pretty there, sweat shiny on his neck and chest, and it was rising and falling so peaceful like. But more'n that, he didn't have no clothes on and, except for the way the picture blocked my view a little, I saw down there. The head on his thing is just as pretty and pink as his lips, and it was just laying there kind of moving a little as his breath went in and out.

Then he kind of turned his face to the side, and I saw his face was wet, but it wasn't sweat. Then he kissed that picture and reached out and placed it on the dresser.

I should' a left then, walking backwards a few steps, then turned and run. But I couldn't. I wanted to call to him in a whisper, but I didn't do that neither. I couldn't move at all, and I could feel the tears start rolling down my cheeks, and the inside of my chest felt all wet.

I knew he was like me. Somebody as pretty as him—with those cornflower blue eyes and Revlon pink lips and slender hands with no hair on the back of them—had to love somebody, never mind like me it was Uncle Sean I loved, never mind like him it was T.S. 'my man' he loved, who more'n likely got killed over there in Vietnam.

So, I stood there watching him, couldn't take my eyes off his smooth skin, the way the little blond hairs caught the overhead light in his room, and the sweat kind of shiny in the ripples of his stomach, and his chest was rising and falling so peaceful like.

And I knew if he'd let me, I'd lay up next to him in his bed, there. And I wouldn't have no clothes on, neither. Just that thought, just kind of aching to see what it would feel like to kiss his lips, made my boner hurt, until I felt myself having a wet dream right there in my underpants, only it wasn't a dream—what I hear the boys on the bus say they do, only they got to jerk off or something.

I never knew what that was until right then, cause as soon as I wet my shorts, my knees began to shake, and I backed up from Uncle Sean's window and ran off into the yard. As soon as I was out of earshot, I just pulled down my underpants and took hold of myself down there and did like those boys on the bus talk about. But there weren't no pleasure in it, cause I hurt so bad for Uncle Sean.

***

Ever since that night, I just got to see Uncle Sean naked and, since it's so hot, I came up with this idea. There's this stock tank up on the Hill place off the lower south end of the field. So, one day when May and Daddy weren't there, I tell Uncle Sean we ought to go skinny dipping. I say I even did it with my sisters, because there ain't nobody for miles to see us. It was near a hundred degrees and we was hot and sweaty, and I let on as to how I couldn't stand it. So, I tell Uncle Sean we ought to wash off the sweat and the dirt. So, he pulls off his boots and shucks his fatigue pants and I couldn't take my eyes off him, except when I shucked my own boots and pants and peeled off my shorts. I had a boner and ran past him real fast and dove in the water, not caring how cold it was, and then I come up in the middle and swam on my back. He's standing on the bank, naked, and his legs are blinding like, and he's taking a leak, not holding himself, but kind of looking down at it, and I pretend I'm rubbing water out of my eyes so I can keep on looking.

When he dove in, he swam out to where I was, and I stood up in the middle of the tank, gripping the soft mud on the bottom with my toes. The water was up to my chin, and so I could take hold of myself down there without being seen and check to make sure my boner had went down.

So now we swim there almost every day, and every day, he likes to walk around on the bank naked. But finally, like in gym class, I don't get a boner every day, cause I'm sure if I did, he'd get suspicious.

***

We was out working in the cotton patch close to the water tank where old man Hill's cattle drink. It was just a week or so after I went and spied on Uncle Sean. It was just me and him and he was talking about when he was a kid about my age. He said he was lonely, and I told him that's just how I used to feel.

Except now that he was here I said I wasn't lonely no more. It was good to see him laugh. We was chopping weeds from between the cotton stalks, which were about boot-top high. It was hot as the dickens, and we both had our shirts off, and I was glancing at Uncle Sean ever five seconds, and thinking about how good he looked.

So, he grins at me and says, "Not lonely because I'm here? Are you sure you're not about ready for a girlfriend, though?"

I didn't like that question, not one bit, cause I wanted to tell him so bad that I want him and me to be boyfriends, so I just kept chopping weeds for a minute or two, watching my hoe dig into the dirt. It sure was full of dirt clods and you had to be careful when you chopped at a weed that you didn't move one of them clods and make the cotton plant come up with it. When it's watered and cultivated in a few more days, the clods will break down, but Daddy wanted us to get the weeds from between the plants first, cause as soon as he waters, the weeds'll outgrow the cotton and shade it out.

But Uncle Sean, he kept looking at me with a smile on his face, and it made me mad, cause he was acting like a grownup and I already figured he was more my age than he was Mama and Daddy's, and I was near as tall as he was. I'd looked at myself in the mirror a long time the other night and besides my same old face, I looked at my own lips and eyes and hair, and me and Uncle Sean favor.

But he says, "Well? Don't you have a girl friend?"

"Don't want one," I said, finally, looking straight into his eyes and near saying I just wanted him to be my boyfriend.

"Boys your age," Uncle Sean says, "need girlfriends."

But I knew something about him. I'd seen him kiss that picture the other night, seen that picture in the box, too, from T.S.

Then I said something I wish I hadn't, cause it made him look real funny. I said, "Do you think I'm pretty?"

Like I said, he looked real funny for a minute, turning his back on me and walking ahead a little chopping weeds, then looking off out over the field where we'd already been. I followed his look, but kept my mouth clamped shut, cause I knew I was red-faced.

Then all of a sudden he stops and I keep chopping weeds 'til I finally get even with him. I stopped too. And waited.

He fiddled in his pants and fished out an old pack of Camels and his lighter. Then he fishes out one of his home-rolled from the pack, holding it between his thumb and first finger. He holds it out to me.

"Your Daddy calls this devil's weed, Will. Do you know why?"

"I don't," I say. "Why?"

"Because it's marijuana. Do you know what that is?"

I say I do, but I don't care.

"Well, over in Vietnam," he says, looking around as if he's afraid someone will hear him, even though we're like two miles from the nearest jack rabbit, "I got started smoking it, same as the rest of the men I served with."

"So?" I say. "It's just strong stinky tobacco, ain't it?"

He says it ain't. He says, "it makes you kind of drunk, but not really drunk, but that's good enough."

"Then why do you smoke it?" I say.

"Because it dulls things that hurt," he says, smiling, but kind of looking sad, too.

"What kind a hurt?"

"Hurt that I got over in Southeast Asia, hurt that went down deep," he says. "Hurt like you should never have to feel."

It was like a dark, heavy cloud full of hail had moved over us, but Uncle Sean holds me with his eyes.

Then he lights up and I can smell that burning tumbleweed smell, again.

"Will you give me another shotgun?" I ask.

He says no, he shouldn't have done it that night.

"Cause you think I'm just a kid, don't you, Uncle Sean?" I ask him. But he don't seem to of heard me, like when I ask him questions he don't want to answer, he goes deaf. I'm not mad that he won't give me a shotgun, cause I don't care about his home-rolled. But I sure would of liked to get close to his lips, again.

He takes a couple of deep drags off the devil's cigarette, then puts it out on his tongue and sticks it back in the Camel pack.

"Are you feeling hurt now," I ask? "Is that why you just did that?"

This time he smiles, and looks so pretty I can hardly breathe.

"No. I'm not feeling hurt, Will. You asked me an important question, and I just wanted to take the edge off, because it's also a dangerous question."

For a minute, I didn't know what he was talking about. "What question? That you think I'm just a kid?"

Then he pulls me up next to him and puts his arm around my shoulders. I can already feel myself stir down there, but I haven't popped a boner, because I'm afraid.

He kind of hugs me to him, and I can feel how hot and slick his skin is under his arm, and even smell his sweat. It's musty and sharp, and I wish I could just settle into his chest.

"You asked me if you were pretty," he says, not looking at me for a minute, then he does—sideways. "That's the wrong question for a boy. You should ask me if you're handsome. There's a difference."

"Well, am I handsome, then?"

That made him laugh and I watched him, because I knew he weren't laughing at me. "You are a very handsome kid," he says. "Don't you think girls'd be glad to have you as their boyfriend?"

I began to shake, cause I know he knows something, too, and he don't want me to feel how I feel.

"That ain't what I want," I say. I want to tell him I know about his buddy, but I get the notion that it's not a good idea.

I also knew why he said my question was dangerous. So that was it. He didn't want to talk about it. I decided right then that I'd find a way to make him know what I wanted was him to be my buddy, and I guess he was scared of that, only I don't know why, cause he'd been in the army and in a war, after all. What was more dangerous than that?

***

I'm up here in the loft, cause that's where I write. I want to write down things I've figured out.

One. I know Uncle Sean is like me. He had a buddy. He thought his buddy was pretty, and his buddy thought he was too. And his buddy give him a picture of him naked, cause that's what buddies like me and Uncle Sean want. Two. I know what wet dreams are. A year or so ago, Daddy said he wanted to have a man-to-man talk and tells me don't be ashamed when Mama showed him my underpants when she did the wash. It's just part of manhood Daddy said. For a long time, I figured Daddy was right, and so when I woke up in the morning and my underpants was all sticky and smelled like flour paste, I weren't ashamed or red-faced, though of course I never said anything about it, except that one time when Daddy had that talk with me. It helped some.

But now I know how to have wet dreams when I'm awake. All I do is think about Uncle Sean and laying up next to him in his bed without any clothes on. I know how to jerk off, too. So, when I go back to school and those boys, specially old Man Hill's grandkid, start in talking about jerking off, and look around at us younger boys, grinning at us cause they don't think we know what they're talking about, I can grin right back and say I do, too.

I ain't never had any trouble being liked, cause I was always good when we played football and ran around the football field and nobody ever bested me in a fight, cause I can fight good, though I don't like to.

I'm looking out the loft and, now, I can see the green spreading out in the fields, where we got a real nice patch of corn growing a foot a day in this June heat. Most days now it's at least a hundred.

But I like the heat and sweating, and I can just close my eyes and smell Uncle Sean's sweat, like the day he put his arm around my shoulders out in the field.

So, I know things, and I could sure use a shotgun from Uncle Sean, because there're things that make me hurt deep down like he said. And I got to plan how I'm gonna get him to kiss me, cause I do think he thinks I'm pretty, and he's got to be lonely, too.

I can hear everybody out in the yard, and Trinket even came in the barn a minute ago calling me, and I just sat real still cause I know she can't climb up in the loft cause the ladder is rickety and she's afraid of bugs.

Daddy and Uncle Sean are working on the cultivator, switching out disks, and raising the bar, now that the cotton's above our knees. I can see Uncle Sean, and from up here he looks small, though he's just down below me. Daddy makes him do all the heavy lifting, but that's all right. Daddy pulled his back out a couple'a weeks ago. I like it now that they ain't yelling at each other so much. I guess they had to get used to each other and Daddy had to get used to the idea that Uncle Sean was gonna be here for awhile.

It helps a lot, too, because Uncle Sean gets some kind of pension checks, and he bought Daddy a pair of gloves and Mama one of them electric can openers. He give the girls some perfume, too, first time his pension check came in the mail. Only I think May would'a wanted a baseball mitt or something like that. But she acted real excited about the perfume, anyway.

But he took me to town and asked me what I wanted, and I said a *Big Chief* tablet, and he laughed and said okay but you got to pick out something nicer'n that, so I got a pair of gloves like Daddy got.

The thing is, everybody got something except Uncle Sean, and he still looks sad sometimes. So, I been touching him a little more. I used to be afraid to, but like when we're in the pickup and he's driving, I sit a little closer and put my arm on the back of the seat and sometimes drop my hand down on his shoulder. At first, I was giddy about it, but long as he just thinks it's me being a kid, I do it, though I sometimes have to rearrange myself down there, especially when he's looking real pretty.

Three
Awakening

I never said, but my sisters May, Rita, and Trinket all like Uncle Sean a lot, too. And one time when they came back from that birthday party Julie Collins had over at her house, Julie's mother Margie Collins came in to visit when she brung the girls back, and Uncle Sean was in the kitchen drinking coffee and he didn't have on no shirt, and I saw Mrs. Collins' eyes bug out of her head, and she couldn't take her eyes off Uncle Sean even when she was talking to Mama. Like when someone is talking to you, but they've got their head turned at something they're looking at.

And I know Uncle Sean notices her looking, too, cause I was looking at Mrs. Collins looking at Uncle Sean, and Uncle Sean was looking at me and he caught my eyes and kind of rolled his.

I meant to ask him how he felt about that, but he got out of the kitchen pretty fast, and was off in the barn when Mrs. Collins drove off. I bout split my side, cause when she left, she was looking around as she walked off the porch, almost tripping. And I knew she wanted to get another look at him. I don't blame her. I feel the same way.

So, thinking about that, today, I talked to my sisters. We sometimes play Old Maid, cause Trinket likes it, and we were in their room, and Uncle Sean and Daddy were out somewhere doing stuff and

Mama was in the kitchen fixing supper, and I figured I needed to play with Trinket, because she and me are buddies.

The funny thing is, we play Old Maid so much the Old Maid card is all bent, but Trinket gets a kick out of us trying to hide it with the other cards.

Trinket's like Daddy in looks with her black hair and dark eyes, but she's so little for her age, Mama says she looks like a little porcelain doll (had to look up that word, porcelain, in the Webster's). And she took up with Uncle Sean right away and sits on his lap in the living room when we're all watching *Bonanza*. She's only eight years old, so I figure I can talk grown kid's talk with May and Rita, though Rita's two years younger than me. She's twelve and blonde like me, though she's got Mama's green eyes, and she sneaks Mama's Revlon and wears it in the bedroom when we're playing Old Maid. She's kind of pretty, too, with the Revlon on.

Now May is freckled, and she's got red hair and green eyes. She's fifteen and really hates boys. So, I knew only Rita would have a real idea about Uncle Sean, so I asked her when she was drawing a card from me, "Do girls like Uncle Sean?"

Trinket just listens, though she's jittery cause Rita's about to draw the Old Maid. May says, "he's too pretty for a boy," and kind of giggles and says, "but I like him all right cause he can throw a curve ball." May's what Mama calls a tomboy.

Rita's hand is hovering over the top of my cards, but I won't let her bend them down so she can get a look to see which one's got the corner ripped off.

"Do they?" I ask, again, and Rita, she looks at me. "Mrs. Collins sure does. The first thing she asked me when I saw her th'other day at the gas station. How's your uncle? Is he married? How long's he gonna be here?"

"What do *you* think?" I say, trying not to seem too interested like Mrs. Collins was.

Rita settles on a card, but it ain't the Old Maid and Trinket lets out a holler. "Will's gonna be the Old Maid!" She giggles. "Never been married, never been kissed! Will don't know what he's missed!"

"Uncle Sean is too old for girls!" Rita finally says.

"Do you think he's pretty, though?" I say, getting real nervous, cause that's what I wanted to ask all along.

"Pretty?" May says. "Pretty?! That's for girls, Duffus!"

But Rita knows what I mean. "He's bea-u-ti-ful!" She says breaking up the word like that.

By now my heart's pounding, cause I found out what they thought, and they didn't look at me funny. Well, not too funny, cause May was grinning at me like she knew some funny secret.

A minute later, who should stick his head in the door but Uncle Sean, saying supper's ready, and Rita and me start giggling. Trinket runs up to him and he swoops her up. "Guess what, Uncle Sean?" She says. "Will's the Old Maid! Never been kissed!"

I will be, I think to myself, looking up at Uncle Sean. He's had a bath and his hair's all slicked back, and he's wearing a real shirt and dress slacks, and I get this terrible heavy feeling in my stomach, as he carries Trinket out of the room. He's going somewhere and didn't tell me!

So, I sat through supper sneaking looks at him, and he's quiet as usual, but I don't like the way his eyes look. They're sparkly, or something, and kind of far away, like he's thinking about where he's going and what he's gonna be doing. I hope it ain't some buddy he's found when he went into town, and then I think about Mrs. Collins, and I can feel my face turning red, cause of the way she couldn't stop looking at him.

So, when supper's done and Daddy's in the living room and Mama and the girls are in the kitchen, I follow Uncle Sean out to his car. He's real polite, though, which makes me feel all the worse, cause it's like he's treating me like a kid, stopping long enough, cause he knows I want something.

I feel like a kid still in my Levi's and no shirt and barefoot, and stinky cause I ain't had a bath. So, I say, "where're you going, Uncle Sean? How come you didn't – "

I stop cause I sound like a whiny kid.

"Just out for a little while, Will."

"But you're all dressed up," I say. And I think it's like a date or something but I can't ask.

Then he looks at me. We're standing by his car, but he hasn't opened the door yet, though he's got his keys in his hand. His paler-than-blue eyes are so beautiful, I feel my chest heaving and my stomach is all heavy, and I'm a kid. "Will, listen to me...okay?" He says. And his voice is so quiet, it's almost like he's choking on the words he's about to say.

"What?" I say. "Uncle Sean, I ain't a kid like you think. I know things."

Then he shifts feet and I see him nod to himself. "I know you do, Will. I'm just going into Lordsburg. There's this little bar. I can't take you there. You know that."

My chest feels all wet inside, cause he even *wants* to go out, instead of him and me sitting in his car or talking in his bedroom. "Well," I say, "drinking is bad. Daddy says it is, says it's money down the drain."

Then he sort of chuckles. "Your daddy's probably right, Will. I'm not that much on drinking, myself. But sometimes... sometimes I just need to get out and think."

And I think about the night I looked in his window and he was holding that picture and his face was wet, and so then I feel sorrier for him than for myself.

So, a minute later, I smile and say good-bye and head back to the house. I know what I'm gonna do, as soon as everybody goes to bed.

***

Later, I went out the window, again. I didn't even keep the screen latched on my north window anymore, I been out it so many times, cause I sometimes just get out and lay in the grass and look at the stars. I been doing that for a couple of years. But as soon as I thought everybody went to bed, I climbed out the window and headed around to Uncle Sean's room. It was so hot everybody had their windows open, and every screen on the house has the same kind of latch, which comes open with a piece of wire.

So, even in the dark, I could slip it into the screen and push the latch away. And I was in Uncle Sean's room a second later, tip-toeing to the door and pushing it shut without flipping on the light. With the windows open, I would be able to hear a car coming up the road a mile away, so I'd know when Uncle Sean was coming and I could get out.

It weren't wash day, so the sheets on Uncle Sean's bed were rumpled, so he wouldn't know I was even in it. So, I pulled back the covers and slid in and covered my head up. I could smell him. I took a deep breath and pulled his pillow up against me and hugged it, and I could smell him on the pillow, kind of like faint sweat, but also a little of that burning tumbleweed, and I kissed the pillow, pretending I was finally kissing Uncle Sean, knowing his face had laid on the pillow, and maybe his hurt had made tears on it, and his lips had probably touched it. And I just laid there listening for his car and hoping Mrs. Collins weren't at the little bar, or —

***

It seemed like just a minute later, but it wasn't, cause Uncle Sean was shaking my shoulder and whispering. "Will? What're you doing in here!" I could smell his breath and it smelled like beer.

He didn't turn on the light, but I saw his face kind of shiny with sweat and he was real close. I didn't know I was going to, but I grabbed him around the neck, and pulled him on top of me. Maybe it was because he was drunk, but he didn't pull back, and all of a sudden, we were laying in his bed and he got his arms around my back, holding me a lot closer than he did that day in the field with his arm around my shoulder, and even though I didn't like the way his breath smelled, I pushed my mouth against his, and our lips touched, and for just a second, he kissed me back. His lips were a lot softer, even, than they look, and my heart was pounding, cause this was even more'n I thought it'd be.

And just when I thought he was gonna let me kiss him a lot and hold me, he got up off me. And when I sat up and tried to take his hand, he grabbed my wrists, both of 'em, and I came flying off the bed. He's a lot stronger than I thought, though I never thought he weren't strong.

In just a second, I was standing up and my knees were shaking, and he had me by the shoulders, whispering in my ear. He was mad and polite at the same time.

"No, Will. You can't do this. It is not right. Now go on, before anybody hears us. We'll talk tomorrow. Go on, now!"

Four
Disappointment and a Lesson

Uncle Sean didn't smile when I came in for breakfast. He was wearing his fatigues and the ugly green t-shirt and a pair of boots, and Mama was asking him how his night was.

I looked over at him, but he only glanced at me.

Daddy was already out, and the girls weren't up yet. And Uncle Sean said there was a fist fight at the bar and the cops came and broke it up. That was all. But I could tell Mama didn't care about the fist fight, cause she's smiling. "Did you meet any nice women?" she asked him, and I knew he didn't like that question, even though he smiled.

He glanced at me, again, and this time it was a long enough look that I saw he had questions in his eyes, questions for me, and I hoped we'd talk, and I hoped he wasn't too mad about last night.

But Mama said, "Diane Mars is a nice-looking gal, Sean. Maybe she ain't real smart, but she's been bartending there at the *Ojo Negro* for ten years, so she's solid and nice looking, too."

"I met her," Uncle Sean said, and then he looked at me and rolled his eyes, and my heart lifted a little. I hoped it was kind of his way of saying he ain't interested. Then back to Mama, he said, "I met several single women and a couple of married ones, too. But I'm not looking to date, just yet, Arlene."

Mama looked flustered and kind of frowned, and I wondered if she has any notion at all about her baby brother. Then she got up and said she had to start the wash and mop.

A little while later, me and Uncle Sean were moving irrigation pipes from a patch of cotton to a patch of grain. We got side boards on the trailer and piled the 10-foot lengths of pipe into it. They were all muddy and heavy, and we were both sweating and grunting, but Uncle Sean was all quiet and wouldn't look me in the eye, except ever once and again, and those questions were still there.

We finally got all the pipe loaded and were in the pickup and he was driving, going slow, and he looked over at me. I was sitting way on the other side of the seat, not trying to be too close and touch him as I have been doing cause I was afraid he'd be mad at me.

"We got to talk, Will," he said.

"I know," I said. "Where do you want to start?"

He took a breath, and I could hear it was ragged and he was nervous, though I didn't know why, only it made me feel sorry for him. He looked back at the road and I was dying because he's so pretty, the way the wind coming through the pickup lifted his hair, and the way the sweat kind of shone down his neck. And his lips were so pink and puffy looking, I wanted to kiss him so bad.

"Let's start," he finally said, glancing at me, fixing me with his eyes, "with what you were doing in my bed." Then he fixed his eyes on the road, because we were coming to the bridge.

"I just wanted to lay in there for a little while, Uncle Sean. I didn't mean to fall asleep in there."

"But why?!" he said, his voice going a little loud. And it was like being slapped. I felt my face turning red and tears stinging my eyes.

"I just wanted—" I stopped. I had to tell him things, lots of things.

"What?" His voice was gentle again. "I'm not angry with you, Will, but you just don't realize how dangerous what you did is."

"Nobody would a found out, Uncle Sean."

"And when you kissed me?" He said. "What were you thinking?"

I felt a sob start way down in my stomach. "I been dying to kiss you, Uncle Sean. You're so pretty!" I couldn't believe I finally said it, but I weren't sorry.

It seemed like light came shining in through the roof of the cab, cause it got so bright in the pickup just then, lighter than the scalding sunlight all around us, so that Uncle Sean was blurry over in the seat, and I could feel the pickup come to a halt and hear the pipes shift in the trailer.

And Uncle Sean killed the engine. Then he turned in the seat and touched my shoulder, squeezing it. "But why? Do you have any idea what you're telling me?"

My eyes burned with tears. I've never been so afraid, and I was beginning to shake, but I had to tell him the truth. I held onto his hand on my shoulder. "I do, Uncle Sean. Ever since you been here, all I can think about is you. You're beautiful! You got lips like a girl's and I just wondered what it would feel like to kiss you. When you gave me that 'shotgun' I thought we was gonna kiss. And you make me feel all sweet inside."

Then Uncle Sean's eyes got tears in them. "But I haven't done anything, have I," he said, sounding really funny, "to make you think—?"

"No! No, Uncle Sean, you been real nice and polite. I don't know why, but I know all I want is for you and me to be boyfriends, like—"

I stopped real quick, because I was about to tell him something and it would make him mad.

"Don't you think," he said, real gentle, "that you're too young to be thinking about things like this?"

I took a real deep breath, and tried to get my shaking under control. "I don't know what you call it, Uncle Sean. I never dreamed about feelings like those that's been running through me. I hurt so bad, I just had to see what it would feel like."

Then he smiled, but he was still sad. "If it's nothing I did, then what made you think I would want that? What if, last night, when I found you in my bed, and you kissed me, what if I had beaten you up?"

I didn't like that, never even thought about it, but I said, "why would you do that?"

"Because, Will, that's what any guy would do to another one that did that."

But I knew Uncle Sean was lying to me, now, and that made me stop shaking.

"That ain't so," I said. "Because I know things about you, Uncle Sean! I know you had a boyfriend, and his name was Theodore Seabrook, and I know he got killed in Vietnam. It's him in that picture you have on your dresser, and you and him were boyfriends, and that's why you was in that hospital down there in San Antonio." By this time, I was wound up, and I had to get it all off my chest, and this whole time, Uncle Sean was looking at me and the questions in his eyes only grew bigger, and now he was breathing really heavy and his breath sounded ragged, but at least he hadn't stopped touching my shoulder.

So, I went on, "I found things in your room, Uncle Sean. I know it was wrong of me to snoop, really bad wrong, just like it was for Daddy to go in there. But nobody would tell me why you were so hurt! You was in that hospital with wounds, all right, but maybe not from being shot, though nobody would say so. But I could just feel it, and I had to find out. I saw them dog tags, too, in the bottom of the box, and I saw that picture of T.S. signed to 'my man,' Uncle Sean. It was to you. You and him loved each other, so there are boys that won't hit me if I kiss 'em. They'd kiss me back."

Then Uncle Sean said real low, like he was so mad he couldn't talk, "You had no right to go through my things, Will. That was wrong, and it makes me doubt that I can trust you."

"No! Please Uncle Sean, you can. I didn't mean to be bad. I only did it once, honest. And you were so sad. But I did one other thing that was bad," I said.

And I told him what I saw that one night I looked in the window at him. I left out the part about having a wet dream, though.

By now Uncle Sean was looking like something I'd never seen anyone look like, kind of pasty faced, either so mad or so sad, it was nearly like he was sick to his stomach, even his lips were white, and I was sorry I'd made him look like that. It hurt so bad, I took a chance and scooted closer to him and tried to hug him, but he put his elbow up and kept me away.

"Don't touch me, Will," he said, real quiet like. "Give me a minute."

So, we sat there, with the noon sun baking the pickup with a hot breeze coming through the windows. We both got real quiet, and you could hear the crickets or grasshoppers start up in the gramma grass, like loud clacking all around us, and I could hear his breathing slow, and slow, and my heart pounding, because I had hurt him so bad, to make him look so pasty and washed out.

Finally, he took a deep breath, himself. Then he nodded at me. "All right. I don't know how you figured it out from so few things in my room, but you're right," he said. "And now you have to understand that you could turn your daddy and Arlene against me. Your daddy would blow my brains out, Will, if he knew what you know. That day he found that picture of me and Ted, he was already suspicious. All it would take—"

"No!" I said, trying to keep from even thinking about Daddy taking down his shotgun from above the bed. "He wouldn't. You're kin! Mama and Daddy love you!"

But Uncle Sean shook his head. "You're wrong, Will. It's just the way things are. There for a short few weeks, I thought that Ted and I could find that rare kind of happiness that so few gay men find. You're right. We loved each other so much it hurt to be apart for even an instant, and that war tore everybody apart. But it just happened that it was also what brought him and me together. He wasn't killed the way you think, though."

"You mean," I said, "he wasn't shot in a battle?"

Then Uncle Sean laughed, but it hurt to hear the bitter way it sounded. "On no! He was *murdered* by one of our own. It's called 'friendly fire,' but it wasn't an accident."

Uncle Sean was using words that confused me, like 'gay' men and 'friendly fire,' and I remembered that Daddy said 'faggots' but I tried to hang onto what he was saying, the whole time watching his beautiful face go back to normal—instead of pasty white and angry, back to pretty and sad and hurt.

He told me about the way our own American boys took care of other American boys they didn't like, how lieutenants and captains got killed all the time by their own men.

"Nobody gets prosecuted," he said. "It's just called *friendly* fire, because the commanders who run this war don't want to let it out that our boys are miserable and dying uselessly—and killing each other. We're not going to win," he said, looking out the window, as if he were looking out across the desert, back, back to Vietnam, so far away, I couldn't even imagine.

Then he got back to talking about his boyfriend, telling me how Ted was shot one night in their camp as he came out of the latrine, right in front of him, and how he grabbed those dog tags, even though he wasn't supposed to. "I needed something of him, Will, something real that would bring him back when I touched it. So, I stole those tags."

I was crying again, and so was Uncle Sean.

Then he said, real quiet, "you're the first person I've ever been able to tell that to, did you know that?"

I started to answer, but he smiled at me. "Please, Will, never tell anyone about this. It may not seem like it to you, but to most people, but especially other men, being *gay* is something so horrible people won't even talk about it. Do you understand?"

I shook my head, because I didn't. "All I wanted, Uncle Sean, honest, was just to see what it would feel like to kiss you! And I just wanted to know why you are so hurt! That's all. Honest. But I won't tell nobody."

By this time, Uncle Sean was pretty much really calmed down, and he smiled like his old self. "Then I thank you, Will. Just remember, though, it's important to never let on to anybody that you've got thoughts about me like you say."

And then he started up the pickup, and by this time, I didn't care, I moved over next to him and he put his arm around my shoulder, and it was not something that gave me a boner, not us being boyfriends or anything like that, but like when you hug somebody at a funeral, cause that's how I felt, like I was with him to be sorry for his buddy T.S. being murdered.

***

But I still want to kiss Uncle Sean. I just can't get that out of my head.

Five
Midnight Cowboy
& the Two Men

For a few days, I felt bad. Real bad, cause of how I'd slept in Uncle Sean's bed and it made him mad. And then how we kind of had a big fight and he looked all white and his lips were almost white and he cried so much. I laid awake those few nights crying, myself, but I couldn't help feeling like I loved him so much it hurt.

But it was sweet, too, that feeling. The hard part, though, was in the day, when Daddy and Mama started looking at me funny and, at breakfast, Uncle Sean was real quiet, as usual, but I saw Daddy looking at him all suspicious like.

Then Mama got me off in the living room and she said, "There's something wrong with you, Will. Did Sean do something to you?"

"No!" I said, but a little too fast. "Uncle Sean's always been polite and nice to me, even though I'm a kid, Mama."

But she grabbed my chin in her hand, and looked at my face, right in my eyes. She had her cigarette in the other hand and took a drag, then looked back in my eyes. "You're not getting enough sleep, and I see you've been crying."

I didn't say nothing cause she hit the bull's eye, though how she knew I been crying is hard to figure.

But she's my mama and I'm pretty sure she's got eyes in the back of her head and can hear better than the wolf in "Little Red Riding Hood."

So as much as I could, I tried to steer clean of both Mama and Daddy and spend as much time with Uncle Sean as I could. The neat thing was, I think he was a little happier, now that we had our talk. Now, when we're out in the field, or working on something in the barn, and we both know Daddy or the girls ain't around, he tells me things. But he always says I can't tell nobody.

And now, I'm jittery about writing in this tablet so much. I been doing it almost every day, so whenever I finish, I put it back in the sack it come in and tuck it up under the rafters, here in the loft. It's a good thing we don't use this loft no more, but there's moldy hay, even a few bales. But Daddy says it costs more'n it's worth to run milk cows like we used to when I was a kid.

There's also something else I been doing up here in the loft, and that's having wet dreams. I get to thinking about Uncle Sean and writing it down, and since I learned how to have them, I just lay back and let it happen, cause I know the other boys on the bus do, too, and I don't believe that stuff they say about hair in my palms, neither. Only it's kind of sad, me doing this, cause I feel let down afterwards. Least I don't get my underpants sticky at night when I'm asleep.

***

I've got to write this! Yesterday was Saturday and way before dark, maybe five or so, I was heading up to the loft, early. I got all my chores done, which ain't really much, since we shut the water off in the fields and the corn's too tall to chop weeds in. So I was climbing up the ladder, and in comes Uncle Sean and he calls me down. I never told him I go up there near every day, and he don't seem to wonder. So, anyway, he comes into the barn and he's already had a bath and is wearing a real shirt again, and my throat gets all choked up, cause I don't like him to go off without me. But he says "you need a bath, because you and me are going over to Deming to the movies!"

I ain't been to the movies since "Swiss Family Robinson" a few years ago, and just the thought made me happy. "Are the girls already bathed?" I asked, cause I thought we was all going, though Daddy ain't much on movies is why we don't go so much.

But Uncle Sean shakes his head. "It's gonna just be you and me, Will." And I feel sorry for the girls, thinking about doing something neat like go to the movies, and he says "you don't look too thrilled. I thought you'd want to do it. Just you and me."

When that sinks in, I laugh and think why not? Cause they went to Julie Collins' birthday party and didn't seem too broke up that I didn't get invited, and before I know it, I'm hugging Uncle Sean like a little kid.

"Then you better hurry. I thought maybe we'd get burgers once we got there."

So, in about twenty minutes I'm so clean I squeak, and I put on one of my school shirts, one of my favorites if you want to know. I like the way I look in it, and I slick back my hair like Uncle Sean, and I put on my best Levi's and saddle-soap my best boots.

Trinket's crying cause she knows I'm going to the movies and she ain't, but Rita and May say they don't want to go, though I know they're kind of mad, and they tell Trinket, "come on and we'll play dolls with you, and you can be the Mama."

Just as we were leaving, Daddy hands me five dollars and says "your uncle said he was gonna pay your way, but I think you ought to be able to pay for the show yourself." So I take the money and stick it in my pocket, and it kind of hits me, like it was a few years ago with my older sisters when their boyfriends come and picked them up. Uncle Sean and me are going on a date! Of course, I ain't gonna tell him that. And I'm thinking I'm gonna call it a date, sure enough!

But that ain't the best part. All this was just so I could write about how things happened, and how it felt. Because last night, when we went to the movies, I got a little proof that other guys like to have boyfriends. Course I also understood a little of what Uncle Sean said to me a few days ago, how other guys would bust your head open, cause they don't like it.

This is how it happened.

It didn't take us no time to get to Deming in Uncle Sean's '57 Chevy, cause he keeps it tuned. It was still real light out when we headed north up 146 toward Interstate 10, and then it was about twenty minutes to go the thirty miles into Deming. We had the windows down and I was sitting kind of in the middle of the seat, but not close enough that Uncle Sean would get mad and tell me to scoot back over. But I was close enough that I could put my arm over the seat and drop my hand down on his shoulder. This time, I did have a boner, cause I was so happy that we were doing something fun together, instead of working in the fields.

And he might've been a little skittish for me to do that, but he let me. We talked a lot and he told me he knew about this show we was going to see, called "Midnight Cowboy," and I asked him if he'd seen it and he said no, but when he was in Lordsburg that night he heard some of the people at the bar talking about it, cause they'd seen it and walked out in the middle of it cause they said it was a little too queer for them.

I got this funny feeling in my stomach at that word, cause kids call each other queer, though I never knew what they really meant, but I had a kind of uneasy feeling it was kind of like I feel about Uncle Sean. But since he hadn't seen it and I hadn't we both just had to wait.

We pulled into Deming just as the sun was setting behind us, and it was one of them clear skies you get out here in the desert, where the blue hangs on in the west for a long time after the sun goes down. But tonight, there was a full moon coming up over them Florida mountains, and my heart was beating fast, cause it was me and Uncle Sean, and in the dusky light as we drove into town, he sure enough looked about as pretty as he'd ever looked, and I had to concentrate real hard on not having a wet dream.

Deming is a big city compared to Animas where I will be going to high school this fall, and it's probably five times as big as Lordsburg, which is why Mama comes over here to shop for school clothes in the fall. So, all the lights were coming on when we headed down the main drag, and we drove right past the Rio Grande theater, where the sign sure enough said "Midnight Cowboy," and we went on through town, and cars were buzzing all over the place, and we ate at the A&W on the east end of town. Just me and Uncle Sean.

Kids with cars and pickups buzzed around the A&W, too, honking and parking and getting out and walking up to each other's cars. The thing is, Deming draws people from that little town of Common east of here, and probably Columbus and Lordsburg and Animas, least for kids that's got money and cars and such. But lots of high schoolers. We play most of them schools in basketball in season, but of course I didn't recognize nobody.

But Uncle Sean looks better to me than any of the guys I see running around and strutting around like they're movie actors. We kept our windows down and Uncle Sean was having a good time, too. Ever once in awhile, playing with me like he's been doing since we had our big talk, he pointed out some girls, and says don't I like them better'n him, and I say no. Then he pointed out a couple of guys, and says are they pretty? And I look and sure enough, they are, but I just have to look at him and say no.

We ate hamburgers and fries and milk shakes, but when I tried to give him my five dollars, he says save it. It's on him. That made me smile, because even if he weren't gonna call this our date, him paying made it like that to me.

Later, we drove back through town and parked in the lot east of the Rio Grande Theater, and this is where I got a little proof. This yellow pickup pulled up and parked next to us and these two guys got out. One of 'em is taller than the other, and he's real pretty with dark eyes and dark hair and real clean looking features. Even Uncle Sean looked in their direction. But this other one, the shorter one is really pretty, like Uncle Sean. He's got the most shiny blond hair I've ever seen, almost like gold, and he looked over at me and smiled, even said "howdy." Then him and the other guy walked off and stood in line, and I'm not making this up, or seeing things that ain't there, the pretty blond threw his arm over the other one's shoulder and even when a car went by and called out "faggots!" it didn't even make the blond guy flinch, except to kind of draw the other one closer.

Then they walked up to two other guys in the line, like they knew them, and as we walked up, I heard the blond one call the other one "babe!"

Uncle Sean and I looked at each other, and I saw he was thinking what I was and heard what I did, cause he smiled real big at me and lightly touched my shoulder.

Anyway, we made it into the theater and got seats right behind the four guys who were friends, and I know they're friends, cause they're sitting together and talking before the movie starts. It was weird, one thing: one of the four guys is really a sissy boy, and pretty like a girl would be and he's with this nice looking man who looked quite a bit older, and while they were talking the sissy guy kind of screeches and I can hear guys behind us say "fuckin faggot" real low like. That made my ears burn, because I knew that word, too, and it's like "queer," and I think it's supposed to mean the same thing, which I didn't know until right then. And then I thought about what my sister May said about Daddy telling Uncle Sean him and his friend in the picture looked like faggots, and I understood right then why Uncle Sean is so afraid that Mama and Daddy would get mad if Uncle Sean was to do something to me.

"Midnight Cowboy" made me nervous, especially when Ratso or something like that tells the cowboy Buck to pick up these hookers. And all the time I know that the cowboy really wants a boyfriend, least it felt like that to me, I couldn't be sure. But people in the audience must've thought the same thing, cause they were booing and yelling "faggot!" real loud, and people got up and left. But me and Uncle Sean stayed right through to the end. He even let me hold his hand for a minute or two, before he squeezed it and put my hand back in my lap, and I could see him shake his head no. The thing is, the real pretty blond in front of us, just kept his arm around the other guy through the whole movie, and I seen a man's wedding band on his hand like Daddy wears, only it was on his right hand. So when we were leaving, I kept looking at them, and I saw a wedding band on the other guy's right hand, too.

Needless to mention, I had a boner through the whole show, and by the time Uncle Sean and me was back in the car and the guys in the yellow pickup drove off, my boner was really hurting bad.

This is the sad part. Kind of. Uncle Sean took me to that show for a purpose and, so, on the way home he talked a lot. He drove real slow, too, cause he had a lot to say.

Since it was dark, I asked him if I could sit next to him, and he raised his arm, once we was out on the interstate, and let me sit up against him. But he didn't smell like sweat. He smelled so sweet, I got tears in my eyes. And then he says, "Will, I'm going to let you sit next to me like this, because I've got things that need to be said, and I want you to know I'm not trying to hurt your feelings."

I started crying right off, silent, cause I was scared, and I loved him so much. I didn't want to hear what he wanted to say, cause I was afraid, but he was letting me sit close like I always wanted. My heart was pounding, too.

"I took you to see that show, because I wanted to see first how you felt about it," he says. I could feel his voice inside his chest, and I wouldn't sit up for a second. I laid my head on his chest, even though it was kind of getting his shirt wet.

"I know," I say. "I figured that out real quick, Uncle Sean."

"Then how did it make you feel?"

"Skittish, specially when that old guy wants to pay the cowboy, and he beats him with the telephone, cause I know he's afraid and needs the money. But Uncle Sean, I know the cowboy loves Ratso! I was real sad when Ratso died."

"It's what you're going to face, yourself," Uncle Sean said. His arm around me was warm, and even though it was kind of hot even this late at night with the windows down and the wind blowing through, I liked the feel of his arm around me.

Then I got this idea. "Then what about the two guys we saw in the parking lot? They were boyfriends, Uncle Sean. I seen they even had wedding rings! They didn't look sad."

And Uncle Sean squeezed me real tight. "I saw that too," he says.

"Then how did that make you feel?" I asked him right back.

"It reminded me of Ted and me," he said. "Like those men."

For a minute we were both quiet. So far, Uncle Sean hadn't hurt my feelings a bit, though it made me kind of sad in my chest that the show was so mean on the cowboy, and he was mean to the old man. I knew about what the old man wanted, and I sure didn't want to be like the old man. I told Uncle Sean that.

"But nothing you saw tonight made you feel any different about wanting to have a boyfriend? Is that it?" Uncle Sean said. "You're only fourteen, Will! Surely you can see that being like that is a lonely way to be. I bet if you got yourself a girlfriend this fall when you go to high school, you'll feel completely different in a year."

I still didn't sit up. I couldn't. I was crying a little harder and my nose was running. I wiped it on my sleeve and put my arm around Uncle Sean's chest and hugged him really hard. And he let me, waiting to hear what I had to say.

So, I said, "No, Uncle Sean. I ain't going to have a girlfriend. Thanks for taking me to the show, but I'm darned more sure about how I feel now than I was when you got here Christmas. I've learned a lot. You wouldn't believe what a kid I was when you got here."

He laughed at that and I didn't get mad at him for laughing, because I could hear him agree, even though he didn't say nothing.

"Then if that's how you really feel, Will, I want you to make a promise to yourself. This is important, okay?"

"Okay," I said. "To myself? And not you?"

He shook his head and kissed the top of my head. We were driving real slow and cars were passing us, then big semis huffed passed, one even blowing his horn, because Uncle Sean really was driving like an old lady, I guess. But he said, "No. You make this promise to yourself."

"Okay," I said, again. "What?"

"Right now, you're a bundle of hormones. You've just come through to your manhood, and I suspect you jack off."

I giggled at that. "Is that what you call it?"

He giggled to. "That's one name for it. People call it all sorts of things."

"So, what's my promise?"

He took a deep breath. I could feel his chest rise against my cheek, and I could hear his heart beating a little faster. "Promise not to rush into having sex with a boy, just because you think you need to."

For a minute, I couldn't even draw a breath. In the back of my mind, I knew my feelings were what he called sex. Though I didn't know what two guys could do. I knew what a boy and a girl could do. I'm not dumb about things like that. But the way Uncle Sean put it was like a splash of cold water on my face, and I still couldn't breathe for a minute.

Then I felt my boner. It ached so bad I knew I was going to have a wet dream soon, right there in the car on the way home. "You mean take all my clothes off? I already thought of that, Uncle Sean."

He burst out laughing so hard, I near got thrown up against the steering wheel. We were getting close to the turn off for 146. I sat up just to look around, kind of disappointed that we were halfway home. Then I remembered he said he was afraid he was going to hurt my feelings.

When he calmed down, Uncle Sean turned off the interstate and got us headed down our road home. "You still haven't promised, Will," he said after a minute.

I hugged his chest hard. "I promise," I said.

"And you won't settle for the first boy that comes along, either, will you?"

I didn't know what he meant. And I said so. "Uncle Sean, I have you. I'm not looking for a boyfriend!"

The moon was well above us, by now, and through the windows, past the headlights, out in the desert, everything was blurry and the mesquites and yucca looked like lumps of black against the pale ground. Only a minute or so later, he took a quick turn off on a rutty road that led up to an old ranch house. Nobody had lived there for as long as I could remember. But he pulled up to the yard and cut the lights and killed the engine.

All of a sudden it was real quiet, except for the hoot of an owl in an old dead tree, or under the eaves of the house.

Uncle Sean sat me up, but he didn't push me away. He kept his arm around my shoulder and looked me in the eye. Even in the dark, I saw his eyes and could make out the color of his lips. I also saw that he'd been crying the whole time we was talking.

"It hurts me to tell you this," Uncle Sean said. His voice was so quiet, I got real scared. I knew he was finally going to say something that might hurt—bad.

"Please, Uncle Sean. Don't say it, if it...if it hurts you. You been hurt enough!"

"I have to, Will. I'm sorry. But let me first tell you that I love you so much. You've given me back my heart. When I got here, after losing Ted, I thought I'd never be able to fall in love, again. You have to understand that. Your love for me has helped me more than the drugs I might have taken to dull my pain. Okay?"

I just nodded. I couldn't speak at all. A sob had caught in my throat and just stayed there.

"And seeing those two men at the show tonight helped me a great deal, too. The ones you said were wearing those rings. But your innocence, Will, and your deep feelings, even your own beauty…and you are beautiful, Will. This has helped me find my own heart. I hope you will always understand that."

"I do. Uncle Sean. I will, I mean."

He nodded, then he drew me back to his chest, and hugged me so hard, I began crying, feeling that sob come out.

He took a breath and so did I.

"Will, you have to realize that you and me cannot…we can NOT be boyfriends. First of all, even though you are very mature and feel very deeply about things, I would be the scum of the earth to make love to you. You're only fourteen years old. I'm almost twenty-three. That makes me an adult and you a minor."

"No, Uncle Sean, please!" I said. But he hugged me harder, keeping his face hidden from me over my shoulder.

"I will not abuse your parents' trust in me. Your father would justly have me thrown in jail, if I made love to you, even though you seem to crave it. I've tested you to make sure you know how you feel, and I have no qualms about who Will Barnett is, but I won't say it. You'll have to say it for yourself, when you finally understand what all this means."

"But I know what it means," I said into his chest.

"No. You don't, Will. But there's one more thing that makes it impossible for us, even if you were my age."

"What?"

"We're related to each other. You've said it a thousand times, Will, every time you call me Uncle Sean. I'm your uncle!"

It got real black there in the car up near the old house, out in the desert. So black I knew if I sat up, I wouldn't be able to see. I didn't want to move. I never wanted to leave Uncle Sean's chest.

But he made me sit up again. This time he looked me right in the eyes and when I tried to turn my face away, he put a hand on either cheek and made me look at him. He wasn't smiling. He wasn't about to laugh, and his eyes were so full of tears the moonlight turned them blurry.

I was sobbing like a little kid. I couldn't stop.

Then real gentle like, still holding my face with his warm hands, he said, "Will, promise me you will never tell anyone, ever, that I did this one thing. Maybe it's for you. But it's also for me."

"What?" I said, though I was afraid to know.

He didn't say a word, but laid me back against the seat, and leaned over and kissed me on the mouth. I felt his lips pressed against mine and they were so soft, so warm, and his breath came onto my face, and I kissed him back a little harder, until we were kissing like I never dreamed. He put his arms around me, and I could feel his hand on the back of my head, and I did the same, and we continued to kiss right there in his car. It musta been five minutes that he kissed me, and when he sat up, I pulled away, and my heart felt so light, all I could do was smile and look at him.

It hurt so bad what he'd said. It hurt until I could feel my heart melt and fall down into my stomach. But when we were finished kissing, I can't explain. It was like he got Ted back for just a little while, and I got my wish. I found out what it was like, and I loved it. Loved him.

"I won't ever tell a soul, Uncle Sean. I hope you find another Ted," I said. "I hope I find another Sean."

He started the engine and flicked on the lights and backed around, and we headed home. Then he says real quiet like, "Thanks, Will. Thanks for being the great young man you are. I won't ever forget you. You'll make some man a wonderful mate."

Six
Halcyon Moments...

I ain't a crybaby. I got to say that. I just read through this tablet up to here, seeing how I only got five pages left. I guess I'll use that other tablet Uncle Sean bought me, cause I can't stop writing. It kind a got in my bones.

Anyway, I ain't, but I see where it looks like I cry a lot. Uncle Sean, he ain't no crybaby, neither. Only he had that nervous breakdown over Theodore Seabrook getting murdered and all. No telling what that'd feel like, say, if Uncle Sean got murdered. Hexes! Cross my fingers. That ain't gonna happen! I bet I'd probably go straight to the hospital, too. Only he won't tell me about that. And maybe I don't need to know how it felt. Only that's probably why he was so sad when he come here.

The good thing is, now that me and him kissed the other night and had our talk and saw those pretty men at the movies with their wedding rings, me and Uncle Sean are sure enough buddies. But not boyfriends.

I'm sad about that. But it scares Uncle Sean, thinking Daddy would blow his brains out if we was to take our clothes off together in the bed. And so, I don't want Uncle Sean to be scared.

I guess I'm learning things I never thought about until I started having sweet feelings in my chest for Uncle Sean, like how grownups have to keep secrets.

And I'm a grownup, cause I have to keep it secret how Uncle Sean makes me feel.

I got to mention that, when we was kissing, I had the wet dream, right there in the car, only I didn't tell Uncle Sean. I can't, cause that would make him feel guilty.

Also, I promised us both. I won't have a wet dream with the first boy that comes along. Sometimes it feels so sweet to hurt so bad for something. And I don't guess hurting sweet-like is so bad. So, I hurt bad that me and Uncle Sean can't be boyfriends. But it's so sweet to be so full of that kind of hurt.

Instead, me and Uncle Sean became buddies. I felt like I could show my feelings when we were alone, and he could tell me things he was afraid to before. So, one day we ran the irrigation pipes up near old man Hill's stock tank. The sun was so hot, it scalded all the blue out of the sky. Only there was big clouds off to the west, and the sun drove hot needles into our skin. So that stock tank got to looking really inviting. The water sparkled and we sweated, and finally Uncle Sean just drops his gloves and says come on, we got time for a swim.

So, we just strip down, and the next thing I know we're both standing on the bank of the pond naked, and I pop a boner and Uncle Sean just laughs, only this time I don't hide it from him. Fact is I kind of want him to see it on me, and just thinking about it makes it ache kind of nice. I noticed he had a bit of a boner too, but he turns away, and I pretend like I don't see it.

Then we both dive in and the water's icy. I got Goosebumps, but soon the water feels nice on my hot skin. So, we swam around for awhile, only Uncle Sean keeps his distance, though we're close enough to talk.

"Uncle Sean," I say, finally, cause I been wondering about it. "How do two guys...you know? Do they have wet dreams together if they lay up in bed naked?"

I saw him smile, though he covers it over with a serious look, and I know two things real clear. First, he sees I'm really dumb, but two, he don't want me to think he's laughing at me.

I was kind of embarrassed at my question and him smiling at it, but I'd asked and I waited to see what he'd tell me.

He swam over to me and then floats on his back. And I just tread water, then he sinks down and stands up on the bottom. He's a little taller than me, and so his shoulders were out of the water. But I keep treading water and scissoring my legs, only my boner has gone down since the water's so cold.

I was about to ask my question again, but Uncle Sean says, "Will, I don't think it's a good idea to tell you about that."

"But why not? Uncle Sean, I'm old enough to know. If I ever do meet a boy that wants to be my boyfriend, and we kiss and we like each other, I don't want him to think I'm dumb."

Still, Uncle Sean shook his head. "You are too young, Will. Didn't you promise yourself you wouldn't have sex with the first boy that comes along?"

"I did, and I meant it," I say, but I don't tell him I feel red-faced for asking what two boys do, but more because he won't tell me. "That movie didn't tell me what to do, though, so how am I gonna know?"

Uncle Sean smiles. "You'll catch on, Will. I promise. If I told you, it would be like trying to describe how beautiful a sunset is by saying what causes the red in the sky. It would ruin it for you."

I still didn't think so, but he wouldn't budge.

***

And so, there for awhile, I felt stuck. I wasn't mad at Uncle Sean for not telling me what to do with a boy. I kind of understand. It's just like he won't let me smoke none of his home-rolled. Only I don't think I can wait until I'm twenty-two like he is, specially if my boyfriend is gonna be as pretty as Uncle Sean, only I don't see how nobody can be as pretty as him.

—◊—

Editor's Note
This was the end of the writing in the *Big Chief* tablet by Will Barnett, and even though he had said he was going to be writing in the *Big Chief* tablet his Uncle Sean bought for him, he didn't, as will become clear, later. The letter and the spiral notebook are the only other materials, besides Sean Martin's dog tags, that were in the barn.

Part Two
The Letter

Editor's Note

I have chosen to include the letter as the next document in this unfolding story, even though there is no date on it to verify that it's in chronological order. The text of the letter, however, indicates that Sean Martin left this letter for Will to find and, as a consequence, I believe, set into motion Will Barnett's decisions as to his immediate future. There appears to be a two-year gap from the end of the entries in the *Big Chief* tablet to those of the spiral notebook.

— ◊ —

Dear Will,

By the time you are reading this letter, you and I will have had a chance to say good-bye, because I didn't want to leave without telling you face-to-face. I think too much of you to have left without a proper good-bye, although no amount of explaining in person could alleviate the hurt you probably feel. But I am sure you will have discovered this letter in your hiding place in the barn soon after I left and, by now, you might be able to better understand.

As will become obvious from this letter, I found your *Big Chief* tablet and the writing you had been doing in it. I had noticed that you disappeared every day about the same time. The night I found you in the barn to tell you I was taking you to the movies, I realized the barn is where you disappeared to every day. It was not long after that when I decided to climb up into the loft. I discovered your writing quite by accident, and I want you to know that I didn't invade your privacy, though I did read a couple of the beginning pages before I made myself stop — especially when I saw that you were writing about me. Even if I had never read a word, however, I knew that you loved me as more than a relative. I am both highly flattered by that, as well as rather sad — but not sad in the way you may think.

I am sad because of who you are and of who I am, which meant we could not become boyfriends because we are related by such close blood ties. The least important thing that separated us was the eight years difference in our ages; rather, it is the gulf of experience between your innocence and the terrible, *terrible* psychic toll the conflict in Vietnam had on me. Add to that my experience with Ted Seabrook and the fact that you must be a virgin, and you will come to understand that it also makes a difference.

But I never thought of you as "just a kid," even though you might have thought so. I did have to keep the distance between us out of respect, not only for your parents, but out of respect for you, Will, more than anything else. I simply could not be the instrument by which you lost your virginity. Although some boys give it away with so little regard for the value being a virgin holds, I simply could not take advantage, either of your obsession for me, or your raging emotions, spurred on by the physiological changes your body was experiencing.

Had things been different, Will, I would have been honored for you and me to become "boyfriends," as you so aptly put it to me on several occasions.

I had to grow up fast, once I was drafted into the army and was sent to Vietnam. I did not want that to happen to you, and still do not. As Arlene may have told you, I was inducted into the armed services straight out of high school; but I did get some valuable college credits in the army prior to being shipped over to Vietnam to be an office clerk out in the field. At least the ongoing training I had in the field offices over there supplemented my education.

Yes, I had my duties to patrol the perimeters of our field camp, was taught to handle an M-16, and was trained in combat readiness, in case our encampment was attacked by the Viet Cong. But I was lucky, in a way, too, that I was mainly a desk jockey.

I was also lucky in that most of my time spent in Vietnam was just plain boring, and I was never the sort of "man" who wanted to fight, either on the playground when I was a kid, or in the field of battle. I avoided fights. Unlike you, I was somewhat effeminate as a youngster, and was made to grow into my masculinity in boot camp — either that or be branded and harassed by my fellows.

Only one person saw through my thinly disguised machismo, and that was Theodore

Seabrook, whom I met only four short weeks before he was killed in cold blood. But up until the time I re-met you as a quite good-looking (or as you prefer, "pretty") young man, those were the very best weeks of my life. Ted and I fell in love with each other from the very moment we met. That such love is almost impossible, I do not doubt, and for that I was again lucky. When he stepped up to my desk to report to our colonel for duty, and I looked up from my work, our eyes met, and for a long moment, neither of us could speak. And when he was finished with the colonel, he stopped back by my desk and invited me out on the spot. Somehow, from then on we simply could not stay apart.

The real horror of that was it took no time for the others in our company to pick up on the love we felt for each other. We were blinded by our love for each other. We even slept together the first night of Ted's arrival; neither he nor I could help it.

Yes, I know I told you not to have sex with the first boy who comes along, and I still think that is wise advice—considering your innocence. But that is precisely what Ted and I did. What eventually got him killed was the fact that we had sex as many times a day as we could get by with it. Everywhere. Once we even did it under a jeep in the middle of the compound! It was not quite as exposed as it sounds, but suffice it to say, it was reckless. We did it between tents; we did it in the bushes outside the safe zone on the outer perimeter of our camp, even though Cong had been spotted in the area. We were also fired upon once as suspected Cong and only narrowly missed being shot, until we could identify ourselves.

Ours was an impossible love, Will—Ted's and mine. And I suppose what burns too brightly burns out more quickly. I would have preferred to have met stateside and to have taken things more slowly and privately, but given the time and place of our meeting and our impossibly ferocious love for each other, we were driven to recklessness when we were together, and driven to madness when we were separated.

It could just as well have been me who was shot in the chest by "friendly fire" as it was Ted, since we were walking together, coming from the latrine. Yes, we had even taken to going to the latrine together. This, however, is not as unusual as it sounds. Perhaps in some more stable military environment, like a fort stateside, it would have looked more suspicious, and would have been absolutely frowned upon. Still, it was probably just the thing that finally tipped the mental balance of the coward who took Ted's life. He was never caught. No one even bothered to look.

And of course, Ted's death was the thing that sent me into oblivion. I went crazy, Will. Crazy with grief, crazy with hatred, and what got me the ticket out of Nam, I went suicidal. Lucky, a third time, the colonel really liked me, and he even knew about Ted and me. At least he indicated as much when he visited me in the camp infirmary, when I was pumped up on Thorazine. He was able to break through the haze of my madness and drug-induced state of calm to communicate his understanding. I remember he said: "I'm going to save your life, Corporal Martin, by sending you back home. There, once you are discharged, I hope you are able to find another Ted."

That he said that to me was not a dream — at least I don't think it was. I also found paperwork for disability among my stuff when I got stateside, filled out and signed by the colonel, himself. He did that for me, Will. Without it, I would not have been able to get back on my feet, once I was released from the hospital — nor to help out your parents with a few of the expenses.

I was a mess, as you well noticed. Once you're identified as a nut case by "mental hygiene" (the military equivalent of psychiatry), they hold on to you; so, I drifted in and out of depression and thoughts of suicide there in San Antonio for the final six months of my career as a soldier. And when I came out here, you helped me the rest of the way back. As I said the night we kissed, Will, you gave me back my heart.

I hope you don't think I left so shortly thereafter because I was freaked. Had there been anything in Hachita for me (other than you), I would still be here. But I have things I need to do, important things to me, and I simply cannot do them in the middle of nowhere.

Once I'm settled in an apartment, a phone, a job, and the beginnings of a life, I will get in touch, and then you can come stay with me. But let's allow the smoke to clear, first. Okay?

Now, I'm thinking about things I want you to one day realize, even though right now you can't, because you are probably hurt that I left. Just keep this letter and read it as often as necessary, and one day many more of my words will make sense.

First, both your mother and father are gracious and wonderful people. I spent many summers with them when I was a kid, and your father was always helpful in teaching me things. Sure, he was impatient at times and, at others, so frustrated with the problems that raising a large family entails—the vicious weather that ruined his crops, the money-grabbing bankers (maybe)—that he was sometimes very hard to take. And when I was here this time, I feel that I overstayed my welcome. But please do not hold that against your father. He's getting a little older and, if you haven't noticed, his health is failing. I know he has ulcers. Farming will do that to a person, and he did not need the aggravation that my being here helped exacerbate. It is also true that he sometimes seemed to pick the arguments that we had. The day he decided the picture of me and Ted on my dresser was unsuitable and indicative of something perverse (remember he said we looked like "faggots"), I think he did have a glimmering of my own homosexuality and wanted to protect you from it. That is also why I often kept my distance from you. I did not want to prove to be the very thing your father feared. Again, it was both out of respect for him and your mother, but also out of respect for you. Only please do not think that being homosexual is something I'm ashamed of in any way; but as a famous general once said, retreat is sometimes the better part of valor; and I felt that this was one of those times. Had I foolishly challenged your father's assumptions about me and Ted and that picture, I would have been gone the day we had the fight, and you and I would not have been able to watch that movie together, nor to have our long talk on the way home. And, most importantly, I would never have known what it was like to kiss you! I'm not kidding, Will. As I said that night, I might have been doing it for you, but I also did it for me. And it helped me as much, if not more, than it helped you. So…No. I am not ashamed of my love for men, and you should not be, either. But sometimes, given the way things are in society, it's not a good idea to always be so open.

We do both have that wonderful vision of the two men we saw at the movies in Deming, and I will carry around with me the notion that, even though they live in just as harsh of an environment as you and I, they were brave enough to wear their wedding bands. Perhaps you will be as extraordinary in the years to come.

Second, your mom has stress she keeps well hidden, as well. She knew more about my homosexuality than your father, and, hence, was actually more of a danger to us being friends. You see, when I was a teen, not too much older than you are right now, your mother caught me in one of your wet-dream situations with another boy. Which is why I know to tell you to save yourself by not having sex with the first boy you meet who happens to want it. Losing your virginity is not all it's cracked up to be if there's not also love involved. So, even though your mother has this knowledge of my past, she probably kept it secret even from herself. She and I were raised in a strict religious household, and our father was much more on-the-lookout for such trouble than Roy.

Third, and probably more important in the long-term, Will, is how well you prepare to live the rest of your life. I'm talking about getting a good education. That's also why I left, after coming to stay with your family for these few months. I have the G.I. bill to fall back on, and I plan to use it. While I will be close to thirty by the time I've gotten a degree, if you apply yourself in school, now, you'll be far more ahead of the game when you're my age than I am. So go for whatever courses your high school offers in college preparation. Just because you're the son of a farmer doesn't mean you have to end up being one, unless that's something you want. That's perhaps your father's greatest failing, Will. And that's his distrust or dislike of "book learnin'." Times are changing and people need a good education.

If you haven't fallen asleep with that little lecture, I'm happy. That's why I'm writing you this letter. It's something between just you and me. I'll drop your parents a line and give them a few telephone calls, but you're the most important person in my life, did you know that? Well, you are. You and I are buddies, and when you get out of high school, I hope you will consider coming to stay with me and go to college. I think we could have some really happy times.

It hurt me not to tell you, when you asked me, what two guys do in bed. As I said then, I'll say it now. I don't want to ruin the experience for you by describing the merely physical details. But I will tell you that, yes, Will, it does involve taking off all your clothes and lying next to that person. If you already know what's physically possible between a man and a woman, then it should not be too difficult to imagine what two men can do together. But the most important part—even in the physical encounter—is that you respect the other person. But even more important than *that* is that you respect yourself.

I think I could go on writing forever, but I do have to end this letter somewhere, so I will end it with this. Remember when we were talking about how Ted died, and I told you I had to take something of his that would bring him back to me when I needed him, and I took his dog tags? Well, I'm giving you mine. You've probably already found them.

So, do me a favor, will you? Wear them. The guys at school will think they're neat, but you will know that I'm lying next to your heart.

I know that we will see each other again, someday.

Love,
Uncle Sean

Part Three
The Spiral Notebook

Editor's Note
In reading the spiral notebook, I was struck by how vastly improved Will's writing was—his physical control of the writing instrument, itself, as well as all the other aspects of using the language and adhering to more traditional grammatical norms. So, my job, here, has mainly been to transcribe the work into a computer. Again, I have taken certain liberties to divide the material into chapters for the benefit of the reader.

—◊—

One
Discovery

When Uncle Sean left one hot July morning, just a little less than seven months after he got here, I was hurt and angry, and I didn't take advantage of those couple of hours from when he told us he was leaving until he was standing by his car. I could've visited with him there in his room as he was packing, and I could have tried to make him feel it was okay, but I didn't. Daddy didn't even bother to go out to the car to say good-bye, and I guess Daddy was hurt, as well. His last words that morning to Uncle Sean still rang in the house: "You picked a damned fine time to leave, Sean, do you know that? Just when harvest season is about to start!" And Mama couldn't go out to the car to say good-bye. She was too torn up. The girls followed him out there, and so did I, but after he hugged the girls, he said he wanted to be alone with me for just a minute. So, once they were back indoors, Uncle Sean looked at me, though I could hardly meet his eyes. I could see the tears in his eyes, just like those that were in mine, which I'm sure he saw.

Only my chest was heaving, and I was biting my lips, and I wanted to plead with him not to leave, but I didn't, because even though he wasn't sobbing like a kid and I was, I knew he was hurting bad. I wish now, being seventeen, that I had known how much he needed for me to act more grown up about his leaving, to know he loved me, and to know he just had to get away. Things were too oppressive between him and Daddy, which came about only a short time after Uncle Sean took me to the movies.

I'm not going to write about that, except to say that Daddy heard from Nick Collins that the movie showing over in Deming was nasty and shameful, and it was that which broke Daddy's trust in Uncle Sean. Afterwards, Daddy scrutinized Uncle Sean's every act, especially when he and I might come back from working in the fields and we were laughing and slapping each other on the backs — anything like that was a sign to Daddy that Uncle Sean and I had an unhealthy, perverse relationship.

Back then, of course, I wanted so much more than Uncle Sean was willing to give me, but I stood up to Daddy, too, denying every accusation he made, tromping on him, really, at the least criticism of Uncle Sean. And that's what drove a wedge between me and Daddy, I think, that never went away, even though it has been two years now that Uncle Sean has been gone. I turned fifteen the month after he left and entered high school, and I sometimes wish that I had been just a little older when I first laid eyes on him. Even a year would have made a lot of difference in the way I handled myself when he was leaving, and so it is with a little guilt that I look back on that day.

There were so many emotions raging through me as I stood facing Uncle Sean in the driveway, me wanting to scream out my pain at him, accuse him like Daddy of running away at the worst possible time, wanting to throw my arms around him and hug him so hard I could force him into my heart, and then he would never be gone! But I just stood there sobbing, as he said words I can't recall. And when he stuck out his hand for me to shake, I took it and gave it a little squeeze, but I was so blinded by my own childish hurt, I turned and ran off and didn't turn back even when he called my name.

The last thing I heard before I was out of earshot was him revving the engine on his car. The last thing I saw of Uncle Sean was a funnel of dust as he sped northward toward the interstate.

I didn't go back to the loft in the barn, either, for a very long time. I just couldn't make myself write down how I was feeling. I felt empty inside, as empty as outer space, maybe.

And when school started in the fall of '69, and I entered high school, my excitement was dulled by loneliness for Uncle Sean. I had looked forward to becoming a freshman there at Animas for a long time. Kids from the farms and ranches—boys that is—grew up itching to join the football team, especially. Even though it's a little school in the middle of nowhere, we usually win. We're tough, like the barbed wire we string along the pastures and fields, like the steel of our muscles we get from working from the time we're old enough to walk. Even the sissy boys out here in this vast, harsh desert are as tough as mesquite bushes with thorns that can puncture a pickup tire.

So, I didn't write in the tablet Uncle Sean gave me. I drew hotrods. Daddy and I fought almost daily, too. It was about Uncle Sean, but his name never came up, except at first, when Daddy demanded to know why I was so broken up over him. I wouldn't tell him, except to scream back that Uncle Sean never did anything to me. "You make it sound like Uncle Sean is some kind of pervert!" I screamed.

There were times I wanted to apologize to Daddy, but couldn't, and when he landed in the hospital just after that harvest season and had a third of his stomach removed from bleeding ulcers, I wanted to be gentle on him and tried to say things that would smooth over his own kind of hurt. The best I could do, though, was work like hell when I got home in the afternoons to get everything done that Daddy wasn't able to while he was laid up in the hospital. During those times I cursed Uncle Sean and, alone in the fields when May wasn't there, or frustrated when I couldn't get a part to fit right on the tractor, and Daddy wasn't there to show me how to do things, I screamed at Uncle Sean's ghost, hovering there all around me.

When he called the first time and I knew it was him, I wouldn't go to the phone when Mama called me, saying it was Uncle Sean and he really wanted to talk to me. I only listened to Mama's side of the conversation, hearing her tell about Daddy being in the hospital, watching her hunched over at the counter gripping the phone and trying to keep the sound of her sobbing from getting through to Uncle Sean on the other end.

So, I had a tough first semester in high school. I never was very good in school, and my grades reflected it. I wasn't allowed to join the football team that fall because of it. I was floundering around like a fish out of water, gulping the air, yet suffocating. Or it was more like a tender plant hanging on in a crevice between rocks up in the Hatchet Mountains, whipped by the spring winds, starved for life-giving water, and quickly wilting, and finally being burnt to a cinder by the blast-furnace that is the sun out here.

But the second time Uncle Sean called, I did take it. I didn't want Mama to see that my hands were trembling, but the harder I gripped the receiver, the more I shook, and when I met Mama's eyes, just before I spoke into the phone, she frowned, then nodded, and left the room.

Our conversation was really awkward but, by then, I was so starved to hear his voice I wouldn't get off the phone, even though I was crying.

"I miss you so bad!" I told him. Those were the first words out of my mouth. And I'm sure he said the same thing back, but I didn't hear it.

Then, maybe to gain a little time, he asked how everyone in my family was, one-by-one, and I told him, "Rita's got a boyfriend, May's on the girls' baseball team, Trinket is the top in her class and she thinks she wants to become a veterinarian." Then I told him that Daddy was all right, though he still seemed a lot weaker to me than he ever did, but that May was a great deal of help to me, as always, and that Mama was even working in the field sometimes but she was looking kind of ragged out, so both May and I tried to convince her we could handle the work.

"And how are you, Will? Still angry with me?"

I let this question hang between us for a long while as I thought about it, and I could hear Uncle Sean kind of gulping on the other end, so I knew I had to lie. "No, I'm not angry, anymore, Uncle Sean," I said, though I was fighting back my tears.

"Then you found my letter?" he asked, and I felt stunned. I felt all the breath go out of me and asked, "What letter?"

He was silent for a minute. "Look in your hiding place," he said. "I hope it's not lost."

My mind was racing, my heart pounding, and I was afraid his letter was lost. I couldn't think of a hiding place at first, until I remembered the loft in the barn.

"I know where to look, Uncle Sean!" I said. "I didn't know it was there! I haven't been there in quite awhile."

"Then look!" he said. "I hope it will help."

Too soon, he was saying good-bye all over again. So, to keep him on the phone for just a little longer, I asked what I was dying to know: "Did you find a boyfriend?"

His laughter sounded like old times to me, and I found myself laughing, too, for the first time in a while.

"Not anyone as pretty as you," he said. "But, yeah. I'm dating someone, though he's nothing like Ted — or you. How about you?"

I felt immediately hurt and flattered at the same time. "I haven't looked," I said. "You know there's just a bunch of ugly farm and ranch boys that go to that school."

"Well, you'll find one someday," he said. After telling me he loved me, he said good-bye and I said that I loved him, too.

When I hung up the phone, I felt better than I had in a long time and even though Mama saw that I had been crying, I smiled at her as I raced out of the house, past the girls, who were out working on the flowerbeds, and kicking up dust all the way out to the barn.

I flew up the rickety ladder and once I was up in the loft, I just kind of stopped, my heart beating as I smelled the musty, moldy hay and saw the dust I'd stirred up hanging in the light coming in through the open loft doors.

At first when I reached up into the rafters, I couldn't find anything, and I was afraid mice or something had got up in there and chewed up my tablet, but more importantly that Uncle Sean hadn't left the letter in a safe place and the mice had ruined it. Then I found the Webster's dictionary and brought it out, smiling to myself at its dirty and spotted condition. I set it on the bale of hay I usually sat on, then rummaged around amid the spider webs and stuff until my hand touched the familiar sack. I pulled it out and blew the dust off, wondering if I'd ever read my childish writing, again. When I pulled the sack out, something funny rattled and when I pulled the tablet out and laid it aside, I looked into the sack and immediately got choked up, because Uncle Sean had dropped his dog tags in there. I knew they weren't Theodore Seabrook's tags, because these were flat and in good condition.

I remembered something that Uncle Sean had said, when he stole his boyfriend's tags when he was killed—he had to have something solid to bring him back, and Uncle Sean had done that for me.

But I didn't find Uncle Sean's letter and I was becoming upset all over again. So, I sat down and started reading my own words, nodding when I read some things, kind of choking up as I read others, laughing at my childish way of putting things, and finally deciding that I needed to start writing, again. It had been too long, though I didn't think I would be writing about Uncle Sean.

I was so disappointed that Uncle Sean's letter was just not there! But at least I had his dog tags, and I put them around my neck and tucked them under my t-shirt.

I didn't want to leave. The pen that I'd used wasn't there, though, so I couldn't write, so I picked up the dictionary and thought about taking it back to the house, when I realized that something thick and white was tucked inside.

Two
Growth

"Clarity." I like this word. It's what I began to feel after I read Uncle Sean's letter. I was almost through with the first semester of my freshman year and, up until then, had made a mess of my grades and such. With Daddy being sick and me working harder than ever, I was about to flunk out, and Uncle Sean's letter jerked me back to myself, the kid I'd been just a few months earlier. I knew I couldn't salvage that semester, but the first thing I did was take seriously his advice for me to get a good education.

I still wasn't ready to touch writing about him, again, or myself, but I surprised the hell out of Mrs. Blackmon, my freshman English teacher, when I told her I wanted to save my grades, if there was any way if I wrote a theme about my father, and how his illness had brought a lot of things home to me. She was skeptical, because a lot of kids in trouble with their grades pull that "is-there-anything-I-can-do," crap.

But she agreed, kind of wearily, and said if I could get the theme in by the end of the week, she'd consider weighting it heavily to bring up my abysmal average.

So, I sat in study hall each morning with a new Bic pen, the Webster's dictionary from home and wearing Uncle Sean's dog tags around my neck, lying close to my heart, as he said. I sweated (and even cried) that theme out. I filled up five of those theme books the school likes to use. When I handed them to her over lunchtime, she about dropped her teeth (which was a real possibility, since they're so obviously false) at the length of my theme.

I hung around as she began to read, red pencil poised above the opening line; and then she began marking here and there, glancing up at me sitting on the front row in her empty classroom, her face stern, then smiling, then frowning. Then she put the first book aside and opened up the next one. I was itching to take that first book and see what horrors she had bled onto my work, but I held back.

She stopped after the second one, glaring at me, and my heart (what was left of it, anyway) began heart-attack tapping. I knew she hated it. And she said, "Will, I cannot concentrate with you sitting there boring a hole in the top of my head. I'll have this back to you by the end of the day."

So, anyway, I saw many things with more clarity as I wrote that theme about Daddy. There were many times while writing it that I ached to talk about Uncle Sean; but his words in the letter kept coming back to me, telling me how gracious and wonderful Mama and Daddy are. And I kind of saw that. Only I doubted that Mrs. Blackmon did, the way she glared at me there when she sent me out of the room.

By the end of the day, I was shaking like a jackrabbit that knows it's about to get its brains blown out when you have it in the headlights. And when I went back into Mrs. Blackmon's classroom, she was there along with Mrs. Hendricks, the guidance counselor, and I just about got sick to my stomach with dread. Because the guidance counselor's job is to stick it to bad kids if they've been missing too much school. I hadn't been, but I wasn't really "there" that first semester, anyway.

"Have a seat, Will," Mrs. Blackmon said. She had a very odd look on her old face, but it wasn't nearly as scary as it had been. Mrs. Hendricks hadn't said anything, yet, but she kind of smiled and nodded, as I took my seat.

Then Mrs. Blackmon returned my 5-book theme, but there wasn't a grade on it, and she said, "go ahead, Will, look at some of my comments. I kind of cringed opening that first book, seeing how she'd bled on it so much, I thought sure she would need a transfusion just to be able to get to her car.

She hated it. She marked things in the margins like "agreement in number," "change of tense," "Cap, Cap, Cap," and "delete comma, add period—" all kind of things. But then I saw "excellent," "nice, fresh expression," "surprisingly complex thoughts."

I was confused, and when I looked up she was smiling. Well, maybe grinning is more like it, and I almost burst out laughing because her false teeth looked huge in her mouth and I wondered what it would look like to feed her an ear of corn.

"Do you want to know what I gave you as a grade?" she asked.

I wiped the secret grin off my inside face, even though she still looked funny. "A 'C'?" I ventured, hoping that it might pull me out of flunking.

"No, Will," she said. "I have never seen such raw talent in one of our freshmen before. An 'A' isn't enough for this."

"Then what about my grade for the class?" I asked, hoping I'd average out at a "D."

"To be fair?" Mrs. Blackmon said, kind of ending in a question I knew wasn't meant for me. "I don't think your other work is indicative of what you're capable of. But the other students have to be considered, since most of them have been putting out real effort all year. I'll give you a 'B minus' for this semester."

I couldn't believe it but stayed quiet in case I had misunderstood. Then I caught a glimpse of Mrs. Hendricks and I wondered, again, what she was doing there.

It wasn't but a minute before I found out. She told me that Mrs. Blackmon had let her read my theme, and I felt kind of embarrassed at that, because I said a lot of things about Daddy, and how we fought all the time, lately. And then when he was in the hospital how I couldn't apologize, though I worked as hard as I could in the fields and stuff to keep the farm going.

So, I waited for her to lower the boom. But just like Mrs. Blackmon, she gushed over my writing and she asked me if I thought I was going to be able to perform like I had with my theme from now on. She mentioned the farm work. And I told her I could handle it, because Daddy was getting better.

Then I talked about Uncle Sean and the letter he'd written telling me I needed to think about getting away from here when I graduated high school and going on to college and stuff, and how I might move out to California where he was now living and go to school, and both women nodded their approval.

It was getting kind of late, and I knew if I missed the bus, Mama would have to drive the near sixty miles to come pick me up, and I said so. But I asked if I could think about playing football next year if I could bring up the rest of my grades.

"Football!" both women said, like they were Siamese twins joined at the throat. "I was thinking more of getting you to work on an academic scholarship," Mrs. Hendricks said. "If you can show the same aptitude in the rest of your studies, I'd like to see you move up in your classes, Will. There's still plenty of time. We pride ourselves in the preparation we give our students..."

I tuned her out for a while and nodded and "yes-ma'am'd" and couldn't wait to get out of there and see if I couldn't get my hands on a new fat spiral notebook, because I had a lot of stuff I wanted to write about before it faded from my mind like smoke into the night sky. I touched Uncle Sean's dog tags and thought how I'd like to write to him to tell him how excited I had made these two old ladies.

Then Mrs. Blackmon said she'd like to drive me home, because she wanted to have a talk with my parents, and I was suddenly afraid. What if she was going to get mad at Daddy for being against "book learnin'," because I had put that in there to explain part of why he was like he was.

So I was in agony all over again, though I did kind of begin to like my English teacher as we drove home. She talked about putting me on an accelerated reading program. "Books that everyone should read," she said, "to get a strong foundation in critical thought."

I rolled my eyes at that, pretending I was looking out the window as the dust boiled behind her Chevy Suburban. I was kind of surprised that she had such a big vehicle, since she was a scrawny little thing and was probably really old, at least sixty or something. But she also had a couple of bales of hay in the back, and a saddle, and she told me that she and her husband ran a small ranch just off the Gray ranch, southwest of here. That surprised me, too.

So, when we got to my house, she took control of both my parents, as they seemed to be awed that a teacher would come out special to talk to them. And my daddy was downright nice to her. By the time she left, Daddy was nodding like a jack-in-the-box at what she said, and when she was just a memory still ringing with laughter in the living room and her cup of coffee was still sitting on the coaster on the coffee table, Daddy turned to me and said how he was proud I'd gotten the teacher to give me a good grade for her class.

"If you can handle your chores, Will," he said, "and still make the football team, you can take the extra courses Mrs. Blackmon and Mrs. Hendricks want you to." I noticed the order of the things Daddy said were important, and so that's how I treated them. Farm work first, football next (because every man's son for fifty miles around played football), and school third.

So that's what I did. And that's how I began growing up a little, from what I now see is the sobbing child I was. It was Uncle Sean's letter and me finally talking to him over the phone that kind of got me back on track.

It's funny how English was suddenly enjoyable to me. Mrs. Blackmon and Mrs. Hendricks did put me on an accelerated reading program. And I'm not talking simple books, like the novels English teachers try to get us students to read for the fun we can find in them. They started me on Thoreau and Dickens and Joseph Conrad. They said Conrad didn't even learn English until he was in his twenties, but he became one of the great writers of the English language.

Not that I was going to take things that far. But I had been writing almost every day since I was fourteen, and once I was introduced to some of the basics of grammar and such, I snapped. Things fell into place, and I wrote a lot more than what I had been doing in private. But I'll get to that. I've got to back track and tell how things went before now.

Three
Awakened to Maturity

The next semester of my freshman year, football season was over, and maybe I should've gone out for basketball, like most of the other boys did, but I didn't. I took P.E., though, and got a laugh at all the pimply butts in the shower. What I told Uncle Sean was right. We were just a bunch of ugly farm and ranch boys, and it seemed like everybody broke out in pimples, just like in grade school when everybody lost their teeth.

But Uncle Sean was right, the guys thought my wearing his dog tags was neat, though to them it was neat since it brought the war home. We all had relatives or knew somebody over there in Vietnam, and we all knew the guys who were sent home dead. Sometimes kids broke down when they heard the news—especially the time that Richard Johnson was killed. He was the all-time, most well-known football quarterback in school up to that time and, just like Uncle Sean, he was drafted straight out of high school. Nobody even thought those war protests covered in the news were a good thing. Not in this part of the country, anyway, where you played football, did your duty for the country and, if you were lucky enough, took over the family businesses, or moved away.

We had several star rodeo riders come out of school, too. Only they didn't come back, except when there was a big rodeo or something in Arizona.

I got a taste of the idea that Animas and Hachita and Lordsburg were slowly dying, as more people left than moved in or were born here. But sometimes I had my hands too full to really notice. I worked like hell on the farm. January turned to February and, still, the winds cut through like knives made of ice and I took over the plowing, turning the old stalks under and the new soil up to the top. I was hoping I might be able to just freeze the pimples off, because when I looked in the mirror, I sure got tired of seeing all those puss-filled bumps, and I was hoping that I'd get my clear skin back.

The girls didn't look much better, except that they could cover their pimples over with makeup, and I got kind'a sick the way the scarred and pimpled boyfriend/girlfriend pairs sprang up around school, like it was some kind of *Twilight Zone*, where no matter how ugly or deformed people in this high school became, they thought each other was pretty.

Then, too, it seemed like the guys in P.E., especially, were turning into sex maniacs, and all we talked about was jerking off. It was easy to join in such talk, since I finally knew what they were talking about—really knew, that is, since I had learned how to have wet dreams while I was awake. Only then I knew it was called jerking off. All the guys seemed to be in a frenzy about it, but I just kind of sat back and nearly quit doing it. I began to think that Uncle Sean was right about kind of saving myself for the right boy.

I missed Uncle Sean, and I wore his dog tags day and night, and reread his letter and raced to the phone when he called and when I was in the kitchen, alone, I'd tell him what I'd been doing, and always tell him that, nope, nobody as pretty as him had come along. I always tried to make myself laugh and joke with him, even though sometimes I was sad and gripping those dog tags.

Four
Beginning to Understand and Hope

When I turned sixteen, last year, I looked back to the time when Uncle Sean had come to visit and saw what a kid I was, how immature, how emotional. Now that I'm a junior, and my skin has cleared back up, I try as best I can to look presentable, just in case there's another boy here in school that might take a liking to me. But that seems unlikely, since I know every one of them. Some of them are better looking than when they were freshmen, but I dream of meeting someone really special, someone that grabs me in the guts like Uncle Sean did. Since I got my driver's license and Daddy trusts me with all sorts of things, he's let me take the pickup and go just about anywhere I want. He says a good-looking boy like me ought to be dating, and even Mama puts some pressure on me in that department. They don't like it that I still wear Uncle Sean's dog tags, and Mama even said, "Will, I just don't think your attachment to them is very healthy."

I remembered that Uncle Sean had said Mama knew about him, but was probably keeping it a secret from herself, so now I keep it a secret from both Mama and Daddy that I still wear the tags. There was even one boy at school, Dick Lamb, the hot-shot quarterback last year that eyed me suspiciously in the shower one day after practice. On the team, I was a tight end and one of his best receivers, and even though we worked well on the field, he had this anger (or something) against me for some reason I didn't know why. And he said, "Ain't it kind of faggoty to wear your uncle's dog tags?"

Since I wasn't so emotional anymore and knew exactly what I wanted, which is a boyfriend, I just let his remark roll off me like sweat and soap down the drain. Then when I was drying off, and the rest of the team was more or less finishing up, he tapped Ronald Spencer on the shoulder and got him and a couple of other guys to come up to me. We were all naked, but I noticed just the slightest beginnings of an erection on Dick's little pecker. It was already angling away from his balls.

"What about it, Barnett, are you a faggot for your uncle?"

There had been a lot of racket in the room up until then, but everybody got real quiet, and the four of them, led by Dick, sort of surrounded me. I turned my back on them, and put one foot up on the bench and started drying my butt with the towel, then I looked back at him sideways, looking straight at his pecker, which was now about half mast.

Then I looked up from his pecker, right into his eyes. "No," I said. "I wear my uncle's tags out of respect." Then I looked back down there, which made the other guys look down there, too, and they saw he was growing. "But I get the distinct impression *you* might be interested in *me*."

All the guys broke out howling as they had all seen Dick's half-mast stiff-on.

It wasn't so much that Dick Lamb was trying to start a fight, because I can't recall that any of us on the team ever got into it with our fists. But it might have been his way of fending off his own interest in other boys, to lead the attack against it. It just seems to me that if some guy is too interested in guys who might be homosexual, they have a problem with it, themselves.

Dick backed off real quick when I called his bluff and didn't say anything more about it. But there wasn't a day that went by that I didn't catch him looking at me across the cafeteria, during practice, in the shower, even in class. As long as he kept his distance, that was fine with me. It might've been completely different if Dick Lamb had been half-way good looking, but there wasn't anything about him I wanted to kiss. Besides, I was saving myself for just the right boy, like Uncle Sean said I should. I wasn't going to settle for the first one that came along. I saw what he meant when he made me promise that.

Five
How Things Change

At school, things really improved from my freshman year, and on through my sophomore year. I got a taste of what it would be like to be a good student. I think back to when I just had to have that *Big Chief* tablet to write about Uncle Sean, and then how the teachers reacted to my theme about Daddy. I even got a story accepted in the *Farm and Ranch* magazine Daddy subscribed to, like how ours was the only farm in the Hachita area, what we raised and why, and Daddy sure was proud of that. I was proud of the check for $25 they sent me, too.

"You got a knack," he told me one day, reading the magazine and beamed at me over the dinner table. But he couldn't imagine what you could do with a knack for words—except I could, though I hadn't told him, yet, that I wanted to go to college. We didn't even have to talk about it, because it was understood I'd stay right there on the farm, while the girls would get married and move off. That's just the way it was.

Only at home, things grew worse. Like I said, after Uncle Sean had left, Daddy and I argued a lot, and then when he was hospitalized with his ulcers, he never was quite the same. It wasn't because he didn't want to keep up with the equipment. He couldn't. And I tried, but I just didn't have as much time as I needed. We had quit raising cotton the year before, because all the trailers we used to haul it from south of Hachita to the cotton gins in Animas began to need major work. Axles getting bent and needing replaced, tires blowing out with a load of cotton sitting by the side of the highway for days at a time. The cost of diesel shooting up, out of site. And my sister Rita got way out of control with some boy and she and Mama began fighting all the time like me and Daddy had been.

We just weren't happy, anymore. Maybe we never were, but I was growing up a lot and seeing things that maybe were always the case, only I was too much of a kid to see them, back then.

I figured once I graduated from high school, I'd up and leave like Julianne and Marsha had. I knew a lot of the boys would be taking over their family ranches, and it seemed like ranching wasn't nearly as costly as farming, but I guess I just didn't know the facts of the matter.

And Mama went downhill some, herself, though she wasn't put in the hospital. Just like Uncle Sean, though, I thought maybe she was sad and mad, and she kind of took it out on May and Trinket, because Rita wasn't around to help, any more, except to make sure her own clothes were washed and ironed.

So that's when I took up writing again, every day.

I ached for something to change, even though school was good. I was lonely, again, as I had been right after Uncle Sean had gone away, but with my driver's license, I was able to get out and get away — always, though, only when I had done my chores and things were settled. But those were my restrictions, not Daddy's. I didn't want to leave anything for him to have to do.

With my own spending money, which I'd made by selling corn to the grocery stores and cafés in the area, I could afford gas and so, for awhile, I'd drive to Deming and Common, looking for those two guys in the yellow pickup that Uncle Sean and I had seen that night at the movies in Deming. I don't think I will ever forget what they looked like, together, especially the blond, especially when he smiled and said "howdy" to me when he was getting out of the pickup in the parking lot there at the Rio Grande Theater.

To have gone to the movies in Deming, I thought they'd be from Columbus, Common, Deming, or Lordsburg (though I doubt Lordsburg, since I'd never seen the pickup there, and I go into Lordsburg a lot). And sure enough, they didn't live in Animas. I knew just about every pickup and cowboy in the whole town, since I spent more time there than I did at home.

If I had ever met them, I only wanted to ask how they met and stuff, and maybe how they got to be so brave like they were at the movies that night. The only problem with staying too long in the towns where we played was that my farm work came first. Daddy still wasn't very healthy, and sometimes when it was really hot out, and he'd been working alongside me in the fields, I'd take a close look at his face, and it was kind of gray, and not his usual leathery brown. Which is also why if he yelled at me for something, even if it wasn't my fault, I'd just swallow the hurt and anger, and maybe later mention it when he'd cooled off.

So, on the day of a game, I would get up before the sun came up and if I had chores around the barn, I used the spotlight I'd rigged up over the bay doors so I could see. Mainly, it was changing out the sweeps on the cultivator or switching out discs. During harvest or planting, of course, it was a whole different set of things I had to do. If I had to set the water and move pipes, I just had to work in the dark.

For a few months, I tried to find those two guys, and drove myself crazy, sometimes, and ended up feeling lonelier, lost, and more frustrated than ever. But I never did see them, again.

So, I spent time in places like Lordsburg and Animas and Cotton City. I sometimes took some of my friends, so we could get bored together, but mostly I was a loner, because I wanted a boyfriend, and I couldn't tell that to them. I still wore Uncle Sean's dog tags, but nobody said anything about it, any more.

To make matters worse, even May was pulling away from the family—not like Rita with her boyfriend—but with all her own extracurricular activities, and even though we were still pretty close, as she entered her senior year, we only saw each other at home for short periods. She still worked in the field with me, but she wouldn't tell me too much about her own business and, frankly, when she'd ask me stupid questions about myself, I didn't really want to tell her that I was lonely, and I sure couldn't tell her why.

Six
The Kid on the Bluff

From our fields out north of the house, I could see the new smelter plant being built near a new town they called Playas. It was one of those company towns, built by Phelps Dodge, just for the workers at the new plant. That smelter plant looked like something out of the future, and I sometimes drove to it over some of the dirt roads the ranchers used and watched the plant going up. Sometimes getting in close enough that I could watch the shirtless guys scampering up and down the buildings, close enough to see the sweat glistening off their backs, but too far away to get a good look at their faces. I could hear the clang of hammers on steel and drills and saws—all kinds of racket. And I wondered if there were any guys there as pretty as Uncle Sean.

I also heard talk in high school that so-and-so had got a job over there and was earning good money, though nobody thought the jobs would last—at least not those construction jobs. I would've considered trying to get on there in the summer between my junior and senior years, but not after my senior year, because I still intended to go to college and move out to California where Uncle Sean was living. He and I talked on the phone a lot, but there was something that always made me sadder after talking to him than I was before. It didn't matter, though, because if he didn't call for a month or so, I missed him and couldn't wait to talk to him again.

Anyway, so every free hour or two that I had, I took off from home. Mama worried over Daddy more and more as he seemed to shrivel up. So, she didn't have that joy like she used to, and Daddy slept a lot, looking gray so often that I just couldn't stand it. It was like trying to be the only one in the family to carry on trying to act happy. Rita was hardly ever there. May was usually off with some of her girlfriends on the baseball, soccer, or basketball teams, and Trinket, bless her little heart, she had a friend in one of the Collins girls she stayed with lots of nights. So, our house was too quiet most of the time, unless Mama was fretting about bills or something; that was when Daddy would rouse himself and try to help me with the equipment or even setting the water or driving the tractors — though he was really in the way, instead. Only I sure needed some kind of help.

So, on one of my short little trips across the desert toward the new plant, that's when I met Lance Surfett. It was a sunny but kind of cool summer afternoon, like there were rain clouds blocking out the sun, but there weren't. Maybe off in the west over the Peloncillo Mountains there had been a rain, and the cool air flowed over our own valley. It was the kind of day I liked, and so I drove out toward the new smelter plant and stopped out of sight of the workers and the buzz of activity and hoofed it the rest of the way, hoping to get a closer look.

The sunlight glinted like sun on water off the shiny metal walls of the plant, and the smoke stack that reached high into the desert sky was like a tube of light, the sun was so bright. Still, the air had a cool breath to it, so I walked fast, enjoying the feel of my boots crunching over the rocks and patches of hard ground. And when I got up to an outcropping of rocks where I could climb up and be within a hundred yards of the plant, and sit my butt down, I saw this kid with kind of longish sandy-brown hair, sitting on the flat rock jutting out over an arroyo, knees drawn up to his chin, shirtless, and staring off toward the plant. When he heard me, he looked around and even though the sun wasn't in my eyes, I couldn't focus on his face for a moment, or see clearly.

It was because big purple bruises covered the left side of his face, starting at his eye and ending on the left side of his mouth. His shirt was laying on the rock next to him, and it was spotted (or maybe I should say, splashed) with what I figured was blood. When he saw me, he jumped up and acted like he was about to run, only there wasn't anywhere to run to, unless he jumped off the rock, down into the arroyo, which was at least fifteen feet down. So, he just stood legs apart, braced for an attack and raised his fists.

He was so small, I took him for a kid maybe twelve or thirteen. "Hey, kid," I said, "I'm not going to hurt you." He spat on the ground, keeping his fists up. "I ain't no damned kid, you son-of-a-bitch!" His voice was as deep as mine, and I was surprised, both at its sound, kind of rich and oily, with a slight southern twang, and at his raw language. So I thought maybe he was more my age (I was not quite eighteen). I wasn't afraid of him, since I'm just over six feet, and saw that he wasn't used to fighting, no matter that he had his fists up. For one thing, the way he folded his thumbs under the curl of his fingers was a dead give-away. For another he was so heartbreaking skinny, his ribs showed, and he looked more like a whipped puppy, standing there. I didn't know what to do, but I kept my arms at my side, moving a little closer, since we were still six or eight feet apart.

"Look, I was just coming up here to watch the work down there," I said, cocking my head toward the smelter plant. "I didn't know anybody even knew about this spot."

"Well, you just go on. I ain't in no mood for company," he said, though he dropped his fists, and kept his eyes on me.

I kept moving in a little closer. I couldn't help it. He looked to be in an awful state, and I planned right then to find out why he looked like he'd been hit by a truck and why his shirt was bloody. When I was close enough to get a better look, my heart just caught in my throat at the condition he was in—that, and how downright pretty he was. His eyes were almost violet in this slanting afternoon light, and even though his lips were a little swollen, they were the same pretty pink as Uncle Sean's.

For me, it was kind of like that morning I first laid eyes on Uncle Sean. Not that I was in love with this strange, beat-up kid, but I felt drawn to him in a way

I hadn't been to any of my classmates or guys on the football team. At the moment, I just wanted to hug him, he looked so pitiful.

"I'm Will Barnett," I said. "I live down yonder," I said, looking back over my shoulder. "You can see the smelter from our farm."

For a moment, he just glared at me, then he seemed to kind of sag. When he stuck his hand out, I was surprised and walked the rest of the way up to him. "Lance Surfett," he said, as we shook hands. "My stepfather just up and moved us out to this god-shit-on place." At that, he cracked a smile, then frowned. "I can't believe a hell-hole like this even exists. There's nothing here! How can you stand it?"

"I was born here," I said, getting a better look at the good side of his face, and I liked what I saw. He sure enough was old enough to shave, because it looked like he hadn't shaved in a day or two. That was just about the only thing that made him look like more than a kid, except maybe his eyes. They had seen some hard times. He didn't have Trinket's innocent look—and maybe not even mine. "Since I haven't really been anywhere else," I said, "it doesn't seem as bad as you say it is."

"Well, it is," he said. "We drove for several days, and when we hit West Texas a couple of days ago, I ain't seen not one fucking lake. Not a single goddamned drop of water. It's just sand and dirt and rocks and heat."

"You didn't see the Rio Grande River when you came through Las Cruces?" By now, we had relaxed with each other a little and I just sat down near his shirt to get a better look at it. Sure enough, there was blood on it, though it was dried and caked and brown.

"That was the Rio Grande?" he said. "That was the river I heard so much about in those westerns? Shee-it! It ain't nothing but a creek!"

I didn't know what to say, and when he cracked another grin and sat down by me on my left side, where I couldn't see the bruise, I saw he was pretty. And I mean really pretty, like Uncle Sean, only with darker features.

For a minute neither of us spoke, and I could feel my heart beginning to pound a little, as I looked off toward the plant. Then back at him, then back at the workers climbing around.

"Is one of those guys your dad?" I asked.

"My dad is dead and buried," Lance said, sounding sad. "But yeah. One of those sons'a bitches is my stepfather."

I was reminded in another way of Uncle Sean—not just Lance's beauty, but his anger and his sadness—and all the feelings I had once felt for Uncle Sean came flooding back as Lance and I sat there and talked while we gazed across the desert at the workmen climbing all over the smelter plant like it was some kind of metal anthill.

He told me he was from New Orleans, though he pronounced it *N'awleans*, and I told him I'd never been that far east. Fact was I hadn't ever been out of New Mexico, except when Daddy and I drove over to Phoenix one time to buy a tractor. But that was a long time ago, before Trinket was even born.

"So is your dad—ah—your stepfather just here for the construction?" I asked.

Lance was laying back on his elbows, and so was I, and he was squinting into the sun, and so was I. The light was becoming more golden by then and his face just seemed to glow. He actually grinned at my question, and just then his lips looked so luscious I felt myself getting a little stiff-on.

"We fuckin' moved here for good, as far as that son-of-a-bitch'll tell me."

"So he's going to work in the smelter?"

"Shit, I don't know," Lance said.

"Then you'll be going to school? What grade are you in?"

He laughed at that question. "I ain't going to school. I quit last year, when I was a junior."

I was a little stunned at that. We occasionally had kids quit school, but mostly our families and the schools worked to keep kids from quitting. "But don't you want a good education?" I asked, and wished I hadn't, because Lance sat up like I'd slapped his face.

"What're you, a god-damned detective? It ain't none of your business." Then he sneered at me and I felt hurt. "You talk like some kind of college-educated snob, is what I think. You and your..." then he just kind of fell back on his elbows like his anger had escaped like gas through a pressure valve.

"I didn't mean to make you mad," I said, still feeling a little hurt, though why I should, I couldn't say.

"It ain't nothing," Lance said, smiling at me again. "You ain't been nothing but nice to talk to. I shouldn't of went off on you like that. It's just my stepfather…he's…"

Again he kind of deflated.

I took a deep breath, because I knew I could really make him mad, but I just had to know. "He's the one that beat you up, isn't he?" As soon as the question was out of my mouth, I cringed, waiting for him to blow up at me, again.

But he sat up and curled his arms around his knees, just the way I'd found him, earlier. Then he looked sideways at me, and I could've died for as beautiful as his face looked, just then, and there were tears in his eyes.

"I can't take it, any more, Will," he said. The way he used my name sounded so nice and familiar, like we were long-time friends. I sat up myself and moved up next to him, my heart pounding so hard, I just knew he could hear it, and I put my arm across his shoulders.

At first, he drew back a little, looking at me like I had kissed him or something. But then he laid his head on my shoulder, and I thought I was going to die of happiness right there. All his tough talk and bad language, the way he jumped up and brandished his fists when I'd first come up on him were kid-like things that showed how desperate and emotionally wrecked he was. So I scooted closer to him and drew him tighter against me.

I was awash in feelings that made me begin to shake, and I knew he could feel me shaking, but I didn't care. He was trembling every bit as much as I was, and so we just sat there like that for a long time before he spoke again. "Thanks for that, Will. You're like an angel. You look like an angel," he said, sitting up and smiling at me. I was sorry when he pulled away.

So, I straightened up and looked him right in the eyes. "Maybe I am one," I said, my voice catching in my throat. "Angels are supposed to help people."

Then I had an idea. "It's kind of hot out here. You look like you could use something to drink. You wanna go for a Coke?"

The way he hesitated, I was afraid he was going to refuse, and I felt like my life depended on him saying he would. Don't ask me why. I'd just met the guy. But already, I liked the way he made me feel, like I was about to jump out of my skin.

He was visibly shaking and, even though I wanted to hug him against me, again, I thought it was going too far.

"When did...that happen?" I asked, indicating his bruises, willing him to agree and go with me, trying to get him to say something. Instead, he just kept shaking, as though he were freezing to death.

"Yesterday," he said, finally, in a voice so quiet it was hard to hear. "I ain't been home since."

"You're probably starved. Maybe we ought to go for burgers," I said, getting up. "Did you run away from home, then?"

He got up, as well. He was still shaking, but I think he really wanted something to eat. He picked up his shirt, and I could definitely see that it was bloody, but also dirty and sweat-stained under the arms. When we were both standing, he looked at me, right in the eyes, like he was trying to tell me something by his look, alone. "I was going to run away," he said, "but when I started walking yesterday, I walked for hours and I saw I wasn't getting anywhere. It's like this desert just stretches wider and wider like some kind of trap."

"It does," I said. "You'd die of exposure out here in just a couple of days." I began climbing down the rock and he followed. So I kept talking. "My pickup's just over that hill," I told him. "I got plenty of gas and we can drive on into Hachita. You been there, yet?"

"Fuck, no," he said, behind me. "We got into Lordsburg, day before yesterday, then got directions to Playas, and came straight here. At least I got far enough so I can't see it, today."

I told him it was just swallowed up by the small mountain to our northwest, and we wouldn't see it at all going into Hachita. "But it's not really all that far away. Maybe fifteen miles along highway 9."

When we got to the pickup, Lance stopped on the passenger side and, from the way he was standing (though all I could see was his shoulders from my side), I could tell he was taking a leak. I did the same, leaving a rain-drop shaped patch of wet on the sand. Then we both got into the pickup, and the way we were sitting, all I could see of his face was the bruised side.

"So, are you running away? I mean, do you still want to? Won't your mother be worried?"

"That's too many questions," he said, softly. "I think I'll have to think about the whole thing. Only, yeah, Mom will be worried, though she knows that son-of-a-bitch beats me, so let her."

I'd never known anyone whose father beat on them. At least not like Lance's stepfather. My own parents spanked me when I was a kid, and my daddy slapped me a couple of times when I talked back, but I didn't know anybody's parents who hadn't spanked them. And the only time I knew of some kid getting bruises was when the principal whacked kids on the butt for things they did at school. In P.E. they'd show off the welts like they were badges of honor.

But Lance's face looked like hamburger meat, and him being out in the hot sun all day, the bruises were kind of filled with blood or something, because they looked sickening. I hoped it wouldn't scar him. I knew it'd take a long time for them to heal. And then I was worried in case he decided to go back home because, what if his "son-of-a-bitch" stepfather slapped him around again, and hit him on the same bruises? I cringed at the thought and glanced over at him.

He was sitting up against the passenger-side door, though still close enough that I could've easily reached over and laid my hand on his shoulder, just like Uncle Sean used to do me, and the way I used to do Uncle Sean.

We drove over the ranch road I had followed to get back in here. When I got to our field road, I knew I'd have to drive past our house to get out the gate and I hoped Daddy wasn't out looking for me. I'd been gone awhile longer than I had planned. It was already close to dusk, and the sky was darkening a little, turning from its washed-out heat blue to the deep blue of dusk. I also knew that it would take long enough to get into Hachita, eat, and get back home that I'd miss supper, and Mama and Daddy would be worried, and maybe a little mad.

So, as I was coming into the field, I slowed down on the north end. "You know what, Lance?" I said. "I just thought about it. But I think I need to tell my parents I won't be home for supper. Do you mind if I stop at the house for a minute?"

I don't think he realized the fix I'd put myself into, because he just shrugged. "Naw, go ahead. But I'll just wait in the pickup."

"Great," I said, trying to be casual about it, as I picked up speed and drove the rest of the way to the house, my mind spinning with ways to explain why I wasn't going to eat at home, how to avoid mentioning I'd picked up a runaway, especially a kid my own age. All kinds of things needed to be explained—or avoided. I hoped Daddy wouldn't ask too many questions or be too mad that I wasn't going to be home for supper.

***

"You're not going anywhere," Mama said, as soon as I had told her and Daddy I thought I'd go into town and grab a burger. It just so happened that everybody, including Rita, was home and they were all in the kitchen getting ready for supper.

Mama hadn't put her foot down like that in a long time—at least not to me. So I felt stuck, because Lance was sitting out in the pickup waiting on me.

"Well," I said, facing Mama, because Daddy was just sitting at the table with Trinket and not really paying too much mind, "I got somebody in the pickup." Then I turned to Daddy. "I was out looking at the work on the smelter plant, and I saw this kid sitting up on a ledge where I sometimes go. He was lost or something, so I was going to take him into Hachita and buy him a burger."

It wasn't a very good way of explaining things, and sure enough the girls perked their ears up and Mama was spooning mashed potatoes into a bowl, then just stopped, looking out the kitchen door.

"Well, go get him and bring him in. No sense in wasting your money on a hamburger when I got chicken-fried steak."

That was not how I had wanted to handle things, but like I said, Mama was in one of her moods, and she wouldn't have it any different.

So I went back to the pickup, my heart beginning to pound, and I felt embarrassed, because as soon as they got one look at Lance's face and his filthy shirt, I was sure both Mama and Daddy were going to hit the ceiling.

I came up to the passenger-side window. "Uh," I said, then kind of cleared my throat. "I had to tell them I had you out here, because Mama didn't want me to leave since supper's almost ready. Do you want to come in and eat?"

Dusk was almost over and Lance's features were softened by the hazy light, and I just sighed waiting for him to decide.

"You didn't tell them I run away, did you?"

I couldn't remember exactly what I'd told Mama. "I think I said you were lost."

Lance grinned at me. "Thanks, shithead. That sure makes me look stupid."

Lance's remark hurt to the quick, but I tried to act like it didn't. "Well, at least I didn't tell them you were running away from home. So do you wanna come in?"

Lance got out of the pickup, still grinning at me, though I don't think it was from something he found funny, *ha-ha*, but maybe the predicament I had put us both in, because as soon as they saw his face, it was going to be over. There would be questions.

I couldn't have dreamt how things turned out, though.

Seven
Struck Dumb

I should've figured Daddy knew everybody for thirty miles around Hachita, and probably all their kids, because as soon as I introduced Lance to everybody and he was standing in the kitchen with his filthy, bloody t-shirt on, Daddy said, "You're a runaway, ain't you? And I'll just bet your parents moved in from somewhere to work on that smelter plant."

I was standing next to Lance. I couldn't believe how quick Daddy honed in to the situation. In fact, Lance and I were standing so close together, I saw I was almost a head taller than he was, and he could have been my younger brother. That's also probably what Mama and Daddy thought—that he was a young kid—because except for his beat-up face and the grown-up look in his eyes, Lance was little. I could hear him swallow, and it made me feel bad that I'd got him in here.

I was afraid Lance was going to run for it, because as close as I was standing, I knew he was shaking a little, and I knew he was scared, just like when I came up on him out in the desert.

"Yes sir," he said, finally, to Daddy. "I did run away."

"And you ran," Mama said, "because somebody gave you a beating?"

He just nodded at that. Mama was still standing by the sink in the kitchen, and Daddy was still sitting at the table, and the girls had stopped what they were doing and were staring at Lance, and I glanced from face to face, feeling awkward and protective of Lance, and feeling guilty, too, that I had brought him in the house.

"Don't matter," I said, looking at Mama, then at Daddy. "Lance is hurt and hungry, which is why I was going to take him in to town."

"Then you better show him where the bathroom is so he can clean up a little," Mama said. "And dab some monkey blood on his face, before those welts get infected. We'll wait supper 'til you're ready."

When we were in the bathroom and Lance had his t-shirt off and was standing in front of the sink, I said I was sorry for getting him into this mess, but he smiled at me. I was standing on his left side, and his smile looked as beat up as his face and I could feel the tears burn my eyes.

"It's all right, Will," he said. He was holding the bottle of stuff Mama called "monkey blood," and I was holding a box of cotton balls.

"You sure?" I asked. "I don't know what they're going to want to do, though."

"Let's at least eat," Lance said. "I'm about to faint I'm so hungry."

I took a cotton ball out of the box and took the monkey blood from him and soaked the cotton ball. Then, as he looked up at me with his face to the light over the sink, I dabbed his bruises. Some of them were puffy and purple. He shut his eyes and winced as I touched his face. I almost jumped when he put his hand on my chest and moved a little closer to me. And I did the same, so that in an instant, we were pressed up against each other, right there in the bathroom, as I dabbed his face with the cotton ball.

A moment later, I set the box down and curled my arm around his naked back, so I could hug him to me. We were both shaking, and I could feel his heart beating against my chest, and that's when I knew Lance was the boy I'd been hoping for, and he was like me and Uncle Sean.

I hated to let him go, but I needed to get him a clean t-shirt, and if we didn't get in to supper, somebody was going to come looking for us.

***

Even though Daddy hadn't been the same since he got his ulcers removed, and was looking worse every year, and even though Mama was more irritable than she had been, since she and Rita fought most of the time, they seemed to pull out of their own problems that night at supper, because Lance presented them a problem like they'd never had to deal with as far as I knew.

Even Rita was involved more with the family that night than I had seen her for awhile. Of course, May and Trinket were their normal selves. Except May was quiet and taking in things the rest of us probably didn't notice; but Trinket was a little angel and wanted to sit by Lance at the dinner table, and I think he liked her attention. She was always the friendly little kid, and of course her size made her seem younger than she was, kind of like Lance's small size made him seem younger than he was, too.

So, supper wasn't subdued as it sometimes was when it was just me and the family. The thing I couldn't have dreamed of is that both Mama and Daddy were reluctant to contact Lance's parents—at least until they'd had a chance to think about it.

"Let's give you a couple of days to get to feeling better," Daddy said, to which Mama agreed. "You can sleep in the girls' old room," she said. I would have called it Sean's room, even if he had only been there a short time, because his absence still filled that room, just like it did my heart.

Lance ate his weight in chicken-fried steak and mashed potatoes and drank iced-tea by the gallon, like he hadn't eaten in a week. Occasionally, over supper, our eyes met, and there were questions in Lance's eyes. Questions I knew involved him and me, the way we'd hugged for a long time on the rock ledge out in the desert, the way we'd pressed our bodies together in the bathroom when I was doctoring his face. So, there was a smile in his eyes, as well, when we looked at each other.

May, Rita, and Trinket helped put clean sheets on the bed in his room, and Trinket hung around long after May and Rita went into the living room to watch television with Mama and Daddy. So, for awhile, Trinket was in the way, and I couldn't talk with Lance by myself. But I really didn't mind, because Lance said he was an only child and told me I was lucky to have sisters.

"Will plays football at school," Trinket told Lance. "He's the star receiver for the quarterback," she told him, and when Lance looked at me with his ruined face, but grinning wildly at what Trinket was telling him about me, I felt embarrassed. He seemed to be looking at me with renewed eyes, only I didn't like Trinket's claim about me being a star, anything.

So, when nine o'clock rolled around and I sent Trinket off to get ready for bed, I was hungry for a little time alone with Lance. I have to admit that, following the way we pressed our bodies together in the bathroom, and after studying him all evening, I was falling in love.

Uncle Sean's advice came back to me over and over, not to give myself to the first boy that came along, but I don't think even Uncle Sean could have foreseen Lance. In the bright overhead light of the bedroom, his beauty filled the emptiness, and I envied the sheets that would enfold him, the pillow he would lay his face on, the warmth he would give up to the bed during the night.

We got to know each other a little better. He avoided talking about his stepfather, and I didn't push. I didn't want to know, except that he said he was ten years old when his mother remarried, following the death of his real father. And the beatings began shortly afterwards.

I could only imagine. It was true how Daddy and I had fought after Uncle Sean left, how Daddy and Uncle Sean yelled at each other, and how Rita and Mama locked horns, too. But there was something completely different to me in the way Lance's life had turned out. He was running away from home, because he couldn't take it anymore. How that would turn out, and what my parents might decide to do about it was something I couldn't know; but I would never have thought of calling my father a son-of-a-bitch. I knew Lance hated his stepfather, and I guess I hated him too, though I didn't know the guy.

Around ten o'clock, when Rita also had to go to bed, over her nightly objections to being treated like a kid, Lance and I went into the living room. May had borrowed the pickup, though, because she said she was going out with some of the girls on her baseball team. It wasn't planned, but Lance and I sat together on the couch, and I even threw my arm over the back of the couch, though Trinket could have fit between us.

Mama was in her platform rocker, and Daddy was leaning back in his easy chair. He didn't look too comfortable, and I wondered if it was because of the situation with Lance being there, or if he was feeling ill. Only I couldn't tell if he was looking gray or not, because when we came in, Mama had turned off the television and didn't turn on the overhead lights, like she might do when we had other company. There was a single lamp turned on next to the television, so the living room was mostly a kind of warm half-light. I don't know if the lighting was intentional on Mama's part, but that way we could all look at each other and talk, and even if our eyes met, the naked expressions were less obvious on either of their faces or mine or Lance's. I think it set Lance at ease a little. It may also have set Mama at ease not to have to look at Lance's beat-up face. The monkey blood made his wounds look all that much worse.

But there we were, sitting in half-darkness and enduring an uneasy silence before Daddy got around to saying what was on his mind. It gave Lance a chance to think through what he might say when he answered one of Daddy's questions. And the darkness hid the fact that Mama and Daddy were studying him from across the room. I knew they were. Just like they had studied Uncle Sean and me.

Lance was skittish, as I had seen out on the rock ledge, and defensive, as when he called me "shithead," though now that didn't hurt at all. I knew a little more about the rough life he'd had. He was coming to us with a whole lifetime of wrecked trust. His stepfather had turned out to be a kind of monster, if you want to know the truth, and his own mother had betrayed him by allowing her new husband to beat him. So I didn't blame him if he might be mistrusting of my parents, maybe even leery of me in a way, but I was going to prove he could trust me.

So, there we sat for a few minutes, until Daddy had taken a few sips of coffee. Then he grunted and kind of sat up, and I knew he must be in pain. "I'm not one to intrude on a man's life," he said to Lance, "so maybe it ain't even none of my business why you're running away from home, but if you were a mind to, I'd kind'a like to know if it's so bad with your daddy or mama that you feel you'd be better off out a there."

I winced, only when Daddy called Lance's stepfather his daddy, because Lance had corrected me real quick. I also cringed at the thought that Lance might use the same strong language he had with me out in the desert. Daddy wouldn't like that.

Lance was quiet for a long moment, though I could tell he was nervous, and I was sitting on his right, so when I looked over at him in the half-light, I just melted, he was so pretty, and I was hoping that he and Daddy would get along. He and Mama, too, but so far she hadn't really said anything.

"When my mom married him, Mr. Barnett, I was real happy, because I missed my father," Lance said, finally, and I could tell he had been trying to get his words just right. "But it wasn't even six months before he started slapping me around, though at first it wasn't in front of Mom. He'd get me off by myself and tell me there was only one man of the house and it sure wasn't a little piss-ant like me."

I winced at Lance's first rough word. But from across the room, Daddy just nodded, though Mama kind of gasped.

"Then the first time he broke my arm," Lance said, I was only twelve, and he told me if I made out like it was him that did it, he'd kill me first chance he got."

I began to shake, listening to Lance, and I was wondering what was going through Mama's head. Daddy's too, but Daddy was a little rougher with people than she ever was, and got in fights when he thought it was called for. Still, neither Mama nor Daddy said anything. I sure was glad the lights were dim, because Lance was shaking so bad the couch was vibrating, and it was all I could do to keep from throwing an arm around him and pulling him close like I had out near the smelter plant.

"But when you're just a kid," Lance said, continuing, "you know you don't have no place to go, and I don't know, I was still hoping Mom would brighten up a little about him, but he was different when she was around, though not for long, because he has a temper and it finally came out when things weren't going all that swift at his job. He finally started beating me in front of her, and she didn't do anything to stop him."

"Did he start beating your mother, too?" Mama asked. I could hear the horror in her tone, and I knew she just couldn't contain herself.

Lance shook his head. "He's yelled at her a few times, real bad, but I guess as long as he had me around to be his punching bag, he was satisfied."

"What I'd like to know, if you don't mind, Lance," Daddy said, leaning forward in his recliner, though it looked like it was an effort. He snapped the foot rest shut under it and rested his forearms on his thighs. "How in the hell could you stand it as long as you did? And you say your mama never tried to stop the beatings?"

I heard a sob start in Lance's throat, and heard him swallow hard, trying to get control of himself.

"She...never. She never once tried to stop him," Lance said, fighting his words. "And when we got out here, and I seen what kind of hell hole he brought us to, and saw he was going to be just as mean as ever, I figured it was time to light out. I should' a done it when I was a kid. But I finally had enough."

"*When* you were a kid?" Mama asked. "You can't be more than fourteen, fifteen at most!"

Lance laughed a little. "I'm small for my age, Mrs. Barnett. I'm almost eighteen years old!"

That was something for them to chew on—Lance's age. I felt like a lug beside him, big for my age, while he was so pretty and little. I noticed he didn't refer to his stepfather by name.

"So, Daddy," I said, when nobody was talking. "Will it be all right, if Lance wants to, for him to stay here? I could sure use the help with harvest just around the corner." I felt stupid for being so quick to mention what I had been thinking, because I should have waited for Mama and Daddy to say what they thought.

"I could sure use a place to stay," Lance chimed in, and for the first time since we began talking, I could hear enthusiasm in his voice, rather than a kind of whipped-puppy tone. I don't mean to make Lance out to be whiny or anything, but I'd never met anyone who had such a hard life. Even Uncle Sean losing his Theodore Seabrook to a cowardly murderer and being hospitalized with suicidal tendencies wasn't as bad as the many years of hell Lance had gone through, and a lot younger, too. I hurt for him so bad, I was glad, again, that the lights were down so low so no one would see my face clearly, because I didn't know what it would show.

We both waited to hear what Mama or Daddy would say about him staying there. All Daddy said that night, though, was Lance could stay there a couple of days. I don't think either of them were too swift on the idea that they might be sticking their noses into someone else's business.

Maybe Daddy would've spent a little more time that night thinking things through, but when he struggled up out of the recliner, I knew he was in pain, and I hoped it was just a passing thing, and that a good night's sleep would bring him around.

Eight
His Name is Lance

Falling in love is so sweet. It's a feeling I can't describe, almost, except that you see the person you're falling in love with and, inside, little strings are tugging everywhere, when that other person smiles, or frowns, or laughs. Lance would look seriously at me, questions in his eyes, and my stomach would flutter, or he'd laugh, and my heart would be pulled. He'd touch me, and I'd feel a tug in my groin.

Those kinds of things. They were wonderful and scary, and like Uncle Sean said, I'd go crazy when I wasn't with Lance.

So, after Mama and Daddy said they were going on in to bed, Lance and I sat on the couch in the living room. We had a lot to talk about, too. It was surprising, though not *really* surprising, if you know what I mean that, as soon as the light went out in the hall and the house was quiet, Lance just scooted over against me, as natural as you please. He was so little, I could get my left arm around his shoulders and my hand reached all the way down his side, and he fit so nice into my body, it was like we were made for each other.

I was kind of nervous about what we were doing right there in the living room, if you want to know the truth, feeling edgy as we sat there, and I kept one ear to the ground listening for any sound in the rest of the house.

"I'm glad your parents are letting me stay for awhile," Lance said. His face was turned up toward me, and I looked down into his eyes. Immediately, I felt tears burn my own. I couldn't believe how we both knew the kind of boys we were, had never even mentioned it to each other, and just pressed our bodies together.

"I'm glad, too," I said, thinking of the night on the way back from the movies when Uncle Sean finally gave me what I'd been wanting when he kissed me and, thinking that, my heart began to pound, and I felt myself getting stiff as a board. It was scary and neat, and I was about to jump out of my skin.

Lance kind of wiggled into my body and laid his face against my chest. "Man, I can really hear your heart beating, like you been running!"

"It's because you're here," I said, kind of choking up. "You do know what I mean, don't you?"

Lance didn't say anything for awhile, but he put his left arm across my chest and squeezed himself against me. "I do," he said, finally. "Do you believe that things happen for a reason?"

"You mean like I just happened to decide to go out near the smelter and you just happened to have been sitting there?"

"Umm," he said, his voice sounding warm and kind of sleepy.

We sat there for a little while. I was content, though my mind was racing and my heart was wearing itself out with joy.

Then Lance sat up a little, though he didn't move away from me. "Well?" he said. "Are you just an angel, or flesh and blood?"

Our eyes met in the soft light of the room, and those questions I'd seen at the supper table were back.

So, I leaned over, bringing both arms around him and very tenderly pressed my lips against his, and he pulled me closer, pressing back with his lips, until we were kissing, and he wet our lips with his tongue and opened his mouth and I opened mine, and we traded breath. It was awkward, though, because I was afraid of hurting his bruises, but Lance didn't seem to care and moved so that we were facing each other straight on and we could put our arms around each other.

Uncle Sean's pretty face floated into my thoughts, and the feelings I'd had when he kissed me were there with me, now, as Lance and I kissed, but there never had been as much physical sensation as there was, now, burning my skin, holding Lance, feeling his chest against mine, his arms warm on my back, his lips and tongue, his breath on my face, even the feeling of his clothing.

My lips were numb when we finally pulled apart, our faces were wet with drool, our shirts were soaked with sweat, and my whole body was tingling, wanting more. But I knew that Lance needed to sleep, and I said so.

"I hate to leave you," he said.

"Me too," I said, getting up off the couch and rearranging my clothes. Lance did the same and then I led him into the hall and down to the bathroom, where I set out a towel and shampoo and soap, and got my toothbrush out of the medicine cabinet, along with my razor and shaving cream. We were trying to be quiet with the door shut and the lights on, but I knew the light would show under the bottom of the door, and if Daddy or Mama got up, they'd see the light. So, once everything was ready, I wrapped Lance in my arms and kissed his eyes and lips. "I guess I better leave so you can bathe."

I wanted to tell him I loved him, but I didn't. It was too soon.

"It's been quite a day, huh?" he asked, as I was getting ready to leave.

I just nodded. "You can find your way to bed?"

He nodded, too. "G'night, Angel," he said.

Nine
Nervous & Strange

The next morning, Lance was like the stranger I had encountered on the rock ledge the day before all over again. I thought maybe the night before on the couch was just a dream. He was already in the kitchen at the table when I came in, and when I got my first good look at him in the daylight—at the ruined side of his face, first, then the good side—when he turned to say hi, he was different than I remembered. Oh, he was pretty all right, and his lips were still that same Revlon pink of Uncle Sean's, and his eyes were that pretty violet color, and his hair was sandy-brown, though a little darker than I remembered, but he looked more his age of coming-on-eighteen, rather than the kid I had held close to me.

What little familiarity I'd felt was gone, though not the heart-pounding attraction at his beauty. Or maybe he was projecting a kind of stranger-at-the-table thing, which put this barrier between him and how I felt toward him. I realized just then that I didn't know this guy at all, and it was going to take awhile to know him.

Was it a kind of fear? I remember it took me a long while to even work up the courage to tell Uncle Sean how I felt about him.

Mama said Daddy was feeling bad this morning, as soon as I took my eyes off Lance and got a mug of coffee from the counter. She said it kind of low, and our eyes met, and there were questions in her eyes that maybe put her to wondering just how I came to bring Lance home, or maybe they were questions about Daddy. But I felt like she was feeling a little strange, too, with Lance in her kitchen—a beat-up kid who'd run away from home. And maybe she was asking me what we were doing and if it was wise to harbor a runaway.

Or maybe these were all just my questions.

I glanced over at the table and saw that Mama had fixed Lance a big breakfast, and he was eating it like he was still starved, so when I got my own breakfast that Mama had ready, I sat down next to him on his right side so I wouldn't have to look at his bruises.

"How're you feeling this morning," I asked, salting my eggs.

When he grinned and kind of winked at me, the stranger thing went away a little. "I feel good," he said, then mouthed *"Angel"* without giving it voice, which made me grin and I felt a string being pulled in my chest.

"Your mom's a good cook."

I glanced up then and saw that Mama was watching us and had those questions in her eyes.

"How's your face, though?" I asked, looking back from Mama to Lance, and cutting up my eggs with my fork.

If anything, the bruises looked worse and more swollen, and I was hoping the purple-looking welts wouldn't scar him.

He touched one of the bad ones tenderly with his fingers and winced, and I thought maybe he ought to be taken to the doctor up in Lordsburg. I thought of infection and puss and looked back at my eggs and took a gulp of coffee for the bitterness.

"I've been hurt worse, Will," he said, realizing my concern.

"But in the face like that? Those welts look pretty bad." He just shrugged and sopped up his egg yellow with a piece of toast.

The girls came in one-by-one. Trinket said hello to Lance in a sleepy little voice before she found the pitcher of chocolate milk that Mama had already made. She popped two pieces of bread in the toaster and got out peanut butter and jelly. She was wearing one of my t-shirts that fit her like a nightie. May was dressed in jeans and a t-shirt and boots, and she said hi to Lance and asked him how he was feeling before she got busy fixing her own breakfast. Mama was teaching the girls how to cook, and May didn't like her eggs the way Mama fixed them. So Mama made her own plate and came to the table and sat across from Lance and me.

Then Rita came in. She was always last these days, because she had taken to wearing makeup and wouldn't come to the table until she had on lipstick and stuff, even when she wasn't going anywhere. Mama didn't like it, but Rita had won. She just poured herself a cup of coffee and came to the table and sat down next to Lance on the other side.

She also said hello and asked about his face, and then she asked where Daddy was.

It seemed like that was what Mama was waiting on, and even though Lance was here, she said Daddy didn't look too good at all and that we should try to be quiet.

I couldn't eat at all, hearing that, so I pushed my plate away and drank my coffee.

Mama said Daddy had a bad night, kind of sick to his stomach, though I hadn't heard anything, and I guess I must've slept like the dead not to have heard.

"You ought to take him to the doctor," Rita said. "He's been looking bad to me for several days, Mama."

"He ain't gonna go," Mama said back. "I've tried to get him in there for a check up."

And so the family talk at the breakfast table went, and Lance seemed to take it all in as though he'd never heard such talk, and maybe he hadn't, if it was just him and his mother and stepfather. I couldn't imagine what it would be like with such a small family and having a monster for a father.

So I finally spoke up and told Mama I'd take Daddy in myself if he wouldn't go with her. As it was, I had been taking over more and more of the responsibilities in the last couple of years and Mama listened to me. I had even put in a crop of alfalfa last year where we used to raise cotton, and neither Mama or Daddy objected.

I put in the alfalfa, because I had read where it enriched the soil and would produce for about five years. I also thought hay would be a good cash crop to sell to the ranchers. It took more water than the other crops, but I didn't have to cultivate and make row beds, so it left me a little freer without Daddy's help.

So, Mama's talk of Daddy being sick made all that responsibility come back, and I glanced over at Lance, feeling kind of sick myself, because I knew I had to run the farm and I was hoping that he would be here to help. Only I was afraid, now that Daddy was sick, that Mama wouldn't want the added burden of Lance—because no telling what kind of ruckus his stepfather would raise with the county sheriff's office, or the state police. Everybody knew everybody else in and around Hachita, so it would only be a day or so at most before everyone knew about the runaway kid. And if anybody saw Lance—even Dosier Duffus—they would be able to figure out he was the runaway. Strangers got noticed in this area, so I couldn't even take him into Hachita for a coke, much less the doctor in Lordsburg, if he needed it.

I was wearing a t-shirt and Levi's and for a minute or so, as I sat there half listening to the talk, I was rubbing my chest, so I could feel Uncle Sean's dog tags. And he was right, it brought him back and what had turned out to be my need for his wisdom; even though he was only twenty-five, he seemed to have more real answers to things than Mama and Daddy, sometimes.

After breakfast, Mama and I went into their bedroom, and in the daylight I could see that Daddy's color wasn't good at all. So, I woke him up as gently as I could and told him I was taking him in to the doctor.

He tried to object, and even managed a good bark, but I said, "No, Daddy. Mama and everybody's worried about you, and even if you ain't sick enough for the doctor, you gotta set Mama's mind to rest."

"I jes need to sleep, Will. Go on, now," he said. But even his voice sounded sick, and that did it. I helped Mama put on his pants and pull on a shirt, and I noticed for the first time how one side of his stomach was kind of bloated, like a balloon, and I wondered how long it had been that way. We messed with Daddy, trying to get him dressed, and when we did, he was mad enough to get up and shuffle into the kitchen like an old man. "Least let me have a cup of danged coffee, then!" he said.

The girls busied themselves cleaning up the kitchen and I noticed that Lance was pitching in, though he was really in the way. I smiled that Trinket had latched onto him like she had Uncle Sean, and he seemed to enjoy the attention.

So when it was time to take Daddy to the doctor, I was about to tell Lance that I'd be back later, but Mama took her car keys out of her purse. "You stay here, Will," she said. "Your daddy don't need to ride in that old pickup. I'll take the car."

In a way, I was relieved, because I didn't want to leave Lance by himself with my sisters — not that they wouldn't be polite, but even with all the commotion of getting Daddy up and ready to leave, half my mind and a whole lot of my feelings were focused on Lance.

Deep down, I knew that, at most, we'd only have a few days together, before we had to face either his stepfather or the cops — or both.

***

"How come you don't have no farm animals?" Lance asked, when I was showing him around the farmyard. He and I were by ourselves, and even though I was worried about what the doctor would find wrong with Daddy, and there was kind of a sick feeling in the pit of my stomach about it, I was happy, in a way, too. The girls wouldn't come out in the heat (except maybe May), so I figured he and I could do just about anything we wanted and not have to worry about being seen.

Not that I was going to do anything too fast, too soon. But I wanted to kiss Lance and hold him, if he felt like it. Only there was still that stranger-thing that had risen up in my mind about him, so I was skittish and afraid to lead things in that direction.

"We used to keep a milk cow," I said, as we got on the south side of the barn, "and chickens and rabbits." I'd shown him the long row of empty rabbit hutches still lined up on the north side of the barn, where the sunlight didn't ever beat down.

"But you ain't even got a dog," he said. He was on my right side, and I glanced at his face, and saw that the bruises looked terrible out in the heat, and I was afraid that too much sun would burn his bruises, so I led him into the barn. It wasn't nearly as hot, though kind of stifling.

"We had one once, but Daddy never thought it was much use having a pet to feed," I said. We were standing in the middle of the lower floor, where we kept the tractors and the cotton picker. I'd been working on taking the picker off the old International Harvester tractor and the basket was held up on an A-frame hoist.

What's that?" Lance asked, looking up at the basket, dangling about eight feet above our heads.

"It's a prison where I keep runaways," I said.

Lance laughed at that, then suddenly, he took my right hand in his left. "I can't stand it, any more, Will. You haven't even made a pass at me!"

"I was afraid," I said, turning toward him.

"Since last night?" Even in the gloom of the barn, I could see the violet of his eyes and the purple of his bruises and the pink of his lips. "I thought you knew how I feel about you, Angel."

I didn't know how to explain what I'd been going through since morning, but all that melted away when he moved against me still holding my hand. When our lips touched, it was like sinking into a hot bath, at first almost too hot, then I felt all the tensions melting away, and we just went at it, though I was careful about his left side, where one of the bruises came down to the corner of his mouth.

We pressed our bodies together, and he began to rub his crotch against me. Since I was a head taller, I had to drop down a little to meet it with my own. Through both our Levi's, I could feel that he had a stiff-on, just like me, and we ground our hips into each other, and I began to wonder if we were going to go further. But I had had this dream, ever since I'd seen Uncle Sean in his bedroom with no clothes on of lying with a boy in bed.

I had no idea what we would do if we did end up in bed, but I pulled away, and held both his hands and looked into his eyes at the questions there.

"I want to be in bed with you," I said. "To do that."

He grinned at me with a puzzled expression. "Do what?"

"You know," I said, lacking any of the words to describe something I had no real idea about. "*Be* with you."

He nodded, then, and pressed himself against me. And we started in kissing again, until I was about to burst. Then he pulled away and held my hands and looked into my eyes.

"You're a virgin, aren't you?"

I began to shake a little, and all I could do was nod.

"Then it's going to be special," he said, "when we do it."

"You're not a…a virgin?" I asked, feeling the dread in my stomach churn a little — partly it was still about Daddy, but it was also about Lance.

He shook his head.

We were still holding hands and he began pulling me deeper into the barn, looking over his shoulder as he backed up, then looking back at me. "Where can we sit?"

I led him up into the loft and we sat down on the bale of hay where I usually wrote in my notebook.

Once we were up here, Lance told me about the other guys he'd had sex with, and I didn't like any of it, because it sounded so cold, maybe even sad. And I learned something that morning, up in the loft, where I had written and had my wet dreams…my silly, childish dreams about having a boyfriend.

I learned that Uncle Sean had been trying to protect me from an emptiness so sad, I couldn't even imagine it, until Lance told me his story. The guys he'd had sex with picked him up on the streets in New Orleans, where he hung out a lot, dreading to go home. He said they fed him, because he stayed away from home a lot and was hungry, and he would agree to go with them if they would buy him food, sometimes even put him up for the night.

I didn't even ask what they did with him. I didn't want to know. I wanted to find out for myself. No wonder, when I'd come along and found Lance out in the desert and he was hungry and I offered him food, as well, his old ways just kicked in, and he was willing to have sex with me, as if I was no different than the guys who had picked him up off the street.

It was sad hearing his story, too, because Lance didn't cry about it, or for that matter, laugh or joke about it. It was just something he did. Which made it cold, and the dread in the pit of my stomach grew. I didn't know how I was going to tell him what I was thinking, but I had to give it a try, because I did not want to be like the men who had picked him up. I wanted him to have deep, lovely feelings for me — the way I felt about him.

I was afraid he didn't feel the same way, though. And again, I looked at him like the stranger he was.

We were both sweating like pigs up in the loft, and his welts and bruises didn't look any better, and I wondered if it was bad for sweat to run over them.

So that's how I began to tell him what I'd been thinking—talking about his physical wounds, first, then moving on to those inside wounds that seemed to make him like Uncle Sean.

"Maybe we should put more monkey blood on those," I said. We were sitting face to face and, up here, it was bright and I could see the minute details of the purple welts. I touched his face gently, and he looked into my eyes.

"Does that hurt?"

He shook his head. "Not as much as it did."

Then I leaned over and just barely touched my lips to his, and he kissed gently back.

"Why do you call me 'Angel'?"

"Because you are," he said. I think his smile was genuine, but I needed to push.

"Did you ever call any of those other guys that?"

Something passed over his face. Was it hurt? Surprise? Anger? I couldn't tell, but tears began to form on his lower lids, and he smiled sadly. "Is that what you think?" he said.

"What?"

"That I think of you like the tricks in New Orleans?"

I had never heard the term 'trick,' but I knew what he meant. "Well, maybe," I said. "Because I offered to take you into town for burgers, and I ended up feeding you, Lance. Just like you said about the guys in New Orleans."

He smiled at me, still with sadness around the edges of his eyes. "I guess I can see why you'd think that, then. But no. I didn't think of those others as angels, because they let me know what they wanted right away, and there was always a price. I had to *pay* for my food, Will. Had to *pay* for my bed and bath."

I felt a little better. "So then why do you call me 'Angel'?"

This time he smiled at me without sadness and took one of my hands and kissed the palm, then held it to his wounds. "Because you are."

Ten
Hopes and Plans—Awry

Later on, I took Lance around the fields, just as I had Uncle Sean that December morning. But at least the fields were green, now, especially the alfalfa, which I had planted in the field north of the house. I was really gambling on it paying for itself, without having to put much labor into it. And I have to admit that it sure looked beautiful to me, with its deep green against the browns and purples and pinks of the hills and mountains—all canopied over by the pure blue sky without a single cloud from horizon to horizon. From the north field, we could see the smelter plant etched against the sky.

"I sure hope that son-of-a-bitch is in deep shit with Mom," Lance said. And again, memories of the stranger I'd met on the rock ledge came back. There was deep bitterness and hatred in Lance's voice, and it made me cringe to hear it. Again, his wounds seemed raw like Uncle Sean's.

"In deep because you*r* mom'll blame him since you're gone?"

He nodded, still looking out toward the smelter plant. "I doubt he'll miss a single hour of work. And I'll just bet they fuck like they always do, whether they know where I am or not."

It was like being slapped to hear Lance's hard words. But I didn't blame him. Don't ask me why I never took up cursing. Daddy never did, and neither did Mama. But I'd heard all the hard words like that all my life from the other boys. I just never liked using them.

"Then maybe they won't even send out word that you're missing," I said. "Maybe we don't have to worry about the cops coming—"

"But I could be dead!" Lance said. "You'd think Mom at least would worry, wouldn't you?" This last was not a question meant for me. It sounded like a question he'd been asking himself for a long time. Maybe every night he spent away from home in the beds he'd paid for with his body. I felt tears sting my eyes to realize that he didn't have any love in his life, if he doubted that even his mother wouldn't really care.

He had been sitting on the other side of the pickup from me. We'd been holding hands, though, and it was nice. But he moved up against me in the seat and threw his arms around my neck, trying to kiss me, and I had to take my foot off the gas pedal, and shift down, so I could take him in my arms and hold him.

"They don't care about me, Will. That's the truth. I'd hoped Mom would, you know? But she doesn't. She never did, I guess."

He began to sob into my chest, and I eased the pickup to a stop before I ran off into the field. I held him against me, hard, the way Uncle Sean had done me that night we came back from the movies, when he'd kissed me, and I realized he'd been crying the whole time he was trying to tell me we couldn't be boyfriends.

And now it was my turn to hold somebody like Uncle Sean had done me. Only I wasn't nearly as wise as he was, because I couldn't imagine the pain Lance felt, the kind that would make him doubt his own mother. I couldn't say a thing.

We began kissing again, and I could feel how wet his face was from his tears, just like mine. We smashed our lips together and crushed our bodies against each other, and he ripped at my t-shirt, running his hands down into my Levi's, laying me back against the door, crawling on top of me, kissing and licking my face until my skin was slick, and I kissed him back like that, tasting the salt of his sweat, running my tongue down his neck and into his ears.

But I couldn't stop thinking that this wasn't how we should do it. He had my t-shirt up around my armpits and had pushed Uncle Sean's dog tags out of the way and was licking the sweat from my chest, and the whole time, pulling at my Levi's, trying to get them off. And I held on, trying to match his ferocity, but thinking, *no. No. Not like this*, though I didn't know what we were supposed to do.

I pulled Lance up to my face, and in the glare of the sunlight coming into the windows of the pickup, could see how beautiful he was, bruised or not. I held him a little away from me. His eyes were glazed over with the same desire I felt, and I could have done it right then, out in the field, but I knew what it was that made me stop.

"You don't want to make love?" Lance asked, breathing kind of heavy. "I'm going to burst if we don't!"

I felt calm, now, though maybe not wise as I wanted to be. "I do," I said, laughing a little at my own ignorance and the look in Lance's face. "But not out here. That wouldn't be making love, would it? I'm not going to just..." (I couldn't say 'fuck') "you know...*bang* you and let you leave, Lance. You don't have to be afraid."

"I'm not afraid!" he said, though I knew he was. He was afraid that if he didn't buy my affection with his body as he had all those other men, I would lose interest.

"Well, maybe not afraid," I said. "I didn't mean that. I've got to know that you feel the same way about me as I feel about you."

There was confusion in his face, now, and his breathing had slowed a little. "How you feel about me?"

"Yes. Lance, we haven't even known each other for 24 hours. Can you believe that?"

He shrugged and grinned and pulled my T-shirt down on my chest, then laid his head on my chest. "Tell me what you mean," he said. His voice was muffled, and I felt his hot breath on my skin through the T-shirt.

"I want us to love each other. I promised myself one night that that's how it had to be. It's too sad, otherwise." Even now I could hear Uncle Sean asking me to promise him I wouldn't give my body to the first boy that came along, to promise myself.

Sweat trickled under my armpits. Lance was lying on my chest and wasn't saying anything, but his breathing had slowed to normal, and he hadn't pulled away. So I just waited.

I looked down on his small body, noting how thin he was and remembered how ineptly he had doubled his fists and tried to look menacing out on the rock ledge. Now, he looked vulnerable and small and I squeezed him to me a little closer. I brushed his hair with my fingers, and waited some more.

***

When Lance and I got back to the house it was close to noon. The girls were fixing sandwiches, and just as I figured, without Mama around to make them work in the yard or something they stayed indoors and were nice and cool in comparison to Lance and me—cool in another way, too. I was still worked up from what Lance and I had been doing, and so was he, and it was all I could do to keep my hands to myself.

When I told him how I felt, it took him a while to understand what I was trying to say. I was afraid to tell him that I was falling in love with him, and he was afraid to tell me the same thing, so he lay on my chest for awhile and then he finally looked up at me. There were tears in his eyes.

"I love you, Angel. I don't know how it happened so fast. But I loved you when you put your arm around me five minutes after we met." Then he grinned. "Is that what you wanted to hear?"

It was, and so I told him back, "I love you, Lance."

And for awhile we just kissed gently, though we both had stiff-ons and were sweating and every time he touched me somewhere with his hands it was like a shock of electricity, or maybe more like my skin was sunburned and it was so sensitive his touch almost hurt.

So, when we walked into the kitchen at lunch, May took one look at us and burst out laughing, and Trinket and Rita looked as confused as I felt, but May just grinned, her freckled face and red hair making her look impish. "What have you two been up to!?" she screamed with laughter and, had it been in her consciousness to even think that we'd practically raped each other, she might have screamed in disgust.

"Well, unlike you," I said, feeling my face turn hot, "we've been working, and we're sweating like pigs."

There was some knowing gleam that didn't go away in May's eyes, however, that left me wondering if she knew the truth.

But I didn't have time to wonder because, as soon as we were finished eating, the phone rang, and it was Mama, telling us that Daddy had been put in the hospital over in Deming.

Rita answered the telephone, and she started crying, so it was all I could do to finally get a few words with Mama.

"It's bad, honey," she told me. "Some kind of infection down there. They're going to have to open him up."

"Is it his ulcers, again?" was all I could think to ask.

"They don't know, Will," Mama said. Her voice sounded so far away. "They have to operate, first thing in the morning, so I won't be home, tonight. So, you're gonna have to take care of things."

"Well, when – "

The phone went dead, and so I hung up and told my sisters what Mama said, not knowing any more than they did.

I really did have work to do, but I didn't want Lance out in the heat, because he did look bad, now that May had brought it to my attention. His lips were swollen (and I knew why), but so were those purple welts, and I was afraid they would get worse out in the sun, so I got him to take a bath, and told him I'd be back a little later.

When he was down the hall, I went back into the kitchen. Rita was making cookies and crying and Trinket was crying because Rita was, and May just looked distressed.

"We need to move some pipe," I said to May, and she seemed relieved to get out of the house with her two younger sisters crying and ran to change into her work shoes.

Five minutes later, we were heading out to the grain field, south of the barn.

"What'd you think Lance and I were up to?" I asked, trying to sound casual about it. "You know, when we came in for lunch?"

May was sitting on the far side of the pickup with her arm out the window, looking about as much like a tomboy as I'd ever seen her. I knew she had come, because she knew I needed help, but I could also tell that my question was one she'd been waiting for me to ask, the way she grinned at me, as though she had something funny to share. She was eighteen and had already graduated high school in May, but she hadn't left home like our two oldest sisters. They had married right out of high school. May hadn't decided what she was going to do. All she ever cared about was athletics. Now, especially with Daddy in the hospital, I was glad she still lived at home. She was a help in the field and didn't mind getting dirty, and I had come to depend on her. She looked at me with that same gleam in her eye from lunch. "You *know* what I meant, Will. The only work you and Lance did was work each other up."

It felt like she had splashed cold water on my face, and I found it hard to breathe.

"What are you talking about?" I asked, not daring to look her straight in the eye.

But she laughed. "Oh, Will, for Pete's sake! You never date, and when Uncle Sean was here, you followed him around like a little puppy, and grieved when he left, and maybe you and he never—"

"We didn't do anything!" I said, a lot louder than I intended.

But May just laughed. "Okay! Don't get so fried! You won't be the first boy that's ever experimented, you know."

My heart was beginning to pound so much I thought I was going to have an attack, and my head swam at May's words. But I fought to keep my calm. "Maybe you don't know as much as you think you do, May."

"Maybe," she said. "But I heard Mama and Daddy talking about Uncle Sean one night, if you want to know the truth. That was like the day before Daddy went into Uncle Sean's room. And you *know* what came of that."

"Then how come you never told me before now?" I asked. "It hurt me really bad, because Uncle Sean *wouldn't* do anything with me if *you* want to know the truth."

"See!?" May grinned. "I *knew* you were in love with him."

"Then how come you didn't run tell Mama and Daddy?"

"Because maybe you're not the only one experimenting."

It was like a big, deep canyon yawned open in front of us at the way May was talking and we were both driving head-long into it. I didn't know if I liked the idea of what she'd just said about herself, either.

"You mean with other girls?"

This time May smiled. "Yes! Dossier Duffus! But it's not all that weird among girls. It used to be that my friends and I practiced kissing each other, so we'd know what to do on a date."

"Only you don't want to date boys. Is that what you're telling me?"

"Maybe not," she said. "I'll just have to see. But I'm kind of sure you already know what you want. And when you and Lance came in for lunch, it was so-o-o obvious the way your hair was all messed up and how rubbery your lips looked. They don't get that way unless you've been kissing."

And then a whole lot of things about May came to mind, like the way she said Uncle Sean was too pretty, and the way she took in things at home, quiet but observant, as though she were analyzing things constantly — and even how she was always running around with other girls and not goo-goo over boys the way Rita was, even though Rita was a lot younger than May. But I was too uncomfortable with those thoughts to continue, and so we just poured ourselves into the work, to get it done, so we could get back to the house, soon.

We both wanted to be there in case Mama called. And I didn't want to be away from Lance any longer than I had to.

***

So that afternoon, I didn't do the work I knew I should. I still had to get the combine ready, since the grain was heading out and old man Hill and some of the other ranchers would be wanting to put up the grain in their silos come August. But I was too worried about Daddy to stay away, and I was anxious to see Lance, again. I figured I'd bathe, too, and get nice and clean and shave, and put on some of my Old Spice and brush my teeth. Deep down in my gut, I was excited, in exactly the same place where the dread about Daddy built more and more.

So, we were all in the living room half watching television and half listening for the phone when it rang. It still made me jump. And it was Mama. She told us that they had Daddy on drugs to try to kill the infection, if that's what it was, and that he was resting.

Then Rita's boyfriend came by, and I was kind of relieved that she would go off with him, but kind of worried too that she might not be here if Daddy got worse. Then the little Collins girl came by with her mother and asked if Trinket could spend the night. Everybody looked to me to make the decision, even though I wasn't the oldest—even Marge Collins expected me to make the decision, though she was hesitant when we told her that Daddy was in the hospital.

"Will you kids be all right, then?" she asked. "Too bad Sean's not here anymore," she added, looking around, and making me grin to myself. "You kids need an adult around, times like these."

"We'll be all right, Mrs. Collins," I told her, as we stood by the front door, waiting for Trinket to gather up her things, including a teddy bear she liked to sleep with. "Only could you bring Trinket back early in the morning? I want her to be here when Daddy comes out of his operation."

She crinkled her heavily made-up eyes into a smile, nodding. "About eight o'clock, I think," Mrs. Collins said. She was at least as old as Mama, though I thought she dressed a little younger, and I thought about the way she had gone bug-eyed over Uncle Sean. Lately, I thought she was a little bug-eyed when she looked at me, and it always made me feel kind of funny, since she was so old and married, even though I knew she ran around—or sure acted like she did.

She wrapped her fingers around my upper arm, and I noticed she had long nails that she kept painted a fire-engine red to match her lipstick. She leaned close to me there in the doorway, and I could smell her perfume, like roses dipped in sweat. "Call me if you need anything, won't you, Will? I just don't know if I ought to leave you kids alone. Somebody should have called me up."

"Honest, we'll be all right, Mrs. Collins," I said, again. I was relieved when Trinket tugged my arm, ready to go.

"Say hi to Mama, if she calls, again," Trinket said.

I sighed, as Mrs. Collins drove off with Trinket.

Then it was just me and Lance and May in the house, and it was late afternoon, and May was grinning from ear to ear, when I went back and sat on the couch by Lance. She was sitting in Mama's platform rocker looking across the room at us.

"Don't mind me, boys," May said in a voice like Aunt Bea on *The Andy Griffith Show*, and I knew she was making a dig out of what she and I had talked about.

I was sitting on Lance's left, and he looked confused at May's comment. He had already bathed and even though his bruises still looked bad, his hair was nice and combed and he looked fresher than he had when we came in for lunch, and even more beautiful. I could feel myself getting nervous, because I was sure we'd get into bed together that night. May wasn't going to say anything, and she seemed to be egging us on with her comment.

So, on impulse, I put my arm around Lance's shoulder, though I didn't dare kiss him in front of my sister. But even that small gesture made him stiffen and frown, so I got up quickly and told them I was going to bathe.

"You can go in and watch," May said to Lance, grinning. "I'm sure you'd rather be in there than out here with me."

Lance looked really confused and a little frightened.

"Come on," I said to him, frowning over at May. "I need to tell you some things, anyway." Then I looked straight at May and back at Lance. "Besides, she knows about us, Lance. So, she's going to tease us one way or another."

When Lance and I went into the bathroom, I turned on the water for a bath, getting it as hot as I could stand it and, in just a few minutes, the steam had risen in there, clouding the mirror and making the whole room feel like an Indian smoke hole. The mirror began to runnel streams of water and the air was cloudy when I started undressing.

"You don't have to stay in here," I said to Lance. He was sitting on the toilet with the lid down, and he was sweating, but also grinning at me.

"No, Angel, I'm going to stay with you," he said in his oily and somewhat deep voice. It was still a bit of a surprise to hear such a beautiful, grown-up voice come out of such a small person.

"I don't want you to get too hot," I said, grinning back and pulling my t-shirt up over my head and tossing it onto the floor by the sink. I removed Uncle Sean's dog tags, then, and decided that I had worn them for the last time, though I was not putting him away. I had finally found my own Uncle Sean, the dream that is of Uncle Sean in Lance.

Then I struggled out of my boots, and Lance just watched me, grinning. Our eyes met and he got up suddenly and came over to me.

"Let me help you out of those pants," he said.

That simple statement caused me to pop a stiff-on in an instant, but I stood with my arms away from my body and looked down as he undid the buttons on the fly of my Levi's, one-by-one, slowly, with such concentration, I knew he was savoring that moment. When he pushed them down I stepped out of them, and then he knelt on the floor in front of me and slid my jockey's off, and I popped out of the underwear like I was spring-loaded.

There had been times in the showers at school when one boy or another suffered a stiff-on in front of everyone else but, because being a queer or faggot was something to be ashamed of, we usually just ignored it. It was natural, in a way, I thought, that sometimes our little willies wouldn't behave themselves, especially when we were coming into manhood. Of course, the other guys called it queer if the guy who popped a stiff-on didn't at least turn away and dress as quick as he could.

But this was different, and I was feeling little insects of excitement running up and down my legs, and strings tugged inside my chest and heart, allowing Lance to look as closely at me as he wanted.

I was reminded of the time at the Hill stock tank when I had deliberately let Uncle Sean see that I was excited. It was after he and I had kissed and, even though he had made it clear that it would go no further than that, I felt I didn't have to hide myself.

I reluctantly moved away and turned off the water and stepped into the tub and eased myself down into the water. Lance began ripping his clothes off, as well, until he stood in the steamy room as naked as I was, and I took his hand and brought him into the tub with me.

He was skinny, and his ribs showed in his chest, but he wasn't bony everywhere, and I liked what I saw. He could have been a long-distance runner with his build, and maybe part of why he was so thin was because he probably had run a lot in his life, no doubt running away from his stepfather, maybe running scared through the streets of New Orleans, in one way or another running away from home for a long time. But he had landed here, with me, and as he sank into the hot water, grinning at me from the opposite end of the tub, I leaned forward and put my much larger, more muscular arms around him and pulled him to me.

It was so hot in the tub that even when our bodies touched, whose arms or whose legs were where wasn't that easy to distinguish by feel. But when our lips met, and Lance opened his mouth and breathed into my mouth with a groan of pleasure, I felt his lips and the slick of his face and tasted him, and my whole body began shuddering as I drew him closer. I looked into his eyes, wet and questioning, and kissed him and he kissed back.

I see now why Uncle Sean did not want to ruin such moments for me by trying to put into words what it was like to be with someone—in my case, another boy. Words fail and cannot possibly describe the sheer physical sensations. I was so deeply in love with Lance Surfett, so much with him physically there in the hot bath, I could not imagine anything more full and wonderful; yet we did not make love, only loved each other, learning to trust each other's touch.

We bathed each other and kissed, and plastered out bodies together, and stepped out and dried each other off; and we both knew we were going to wait until later that night to make love.

***

We gathered up our hot, damp clothing and ran down the hall naked to my room, laughing. I was on the lookout for May, but we made it to my room and closed the door. It felt great to be out of the steamy bathroom, and for a little while, even though the sun had not yet set and it was a hot July day outdoors, the air cooled our skin as we stood in my room. I got Lance underwear and a t-shirt from my dresser and got some for myself.

It was then that I realized that if Lance stayed here very much longer, he was going to need some clothes that fit. So, when Lance was dressed in the smallest clothes I could find, I took our dirty clothing, along with a few other things from my hamper and took them into the utility room off the kitchen and threw Levi's, shorts, socks, and t-shirts all together into the Maytag. Lance was with me. We had passed May in the kitchen, where she was finishing up supper for the three of us, and even though she winked at me when we passed by, she didn't make any catty remark, for which I was grateful.

Unlike our two oldest sisters, May wasn't in a hurry to get away from the farm, and she sure wasn't interested in getting married any time soon. So, except for the shadow of Daddy being put in the hospital, and Mama not being home, too, it was kind of a neat evening with just May and me and Lance there.

May and I were the closest in age to each other, and close in the way we preferred working outdoors, but that night, she wanted to talk about herself, and how until now she'd kept her own secrets about the girls she ran around with, and again it felt like we were driving down into a dark canyon without knowing where the bottom was or what we'd find once we got there.

The last thing she said before we turned out the lights and went to bed was, "I'm glad for you, Will. I know how much you hurt, because of the way you felt about Uncle Sean. So, I'll wait up for Rita and steer her off to bed. You and Lance should have at least this one night, together."

So, Lance and I said good-night to May and went off to bed. There are no real words to say how it felt. Was it like a married couple's wedding night? That's the only way I could describe it, though I'm not dumb enough to think that Lance and I are married. We're still strangers, and that's for sure the truth.

Do I love him? Does he love me? I can't even write these words without shaking and feeling that sweet hurt down in my guts about him. I can't keep from grinning from ear-to-ear, either, as I think about my child self who just wanted to lay against Uncle Sean with no clothes on, knowing so very little of what else there was to do when you made love—especially to another boy.

Uncle Sean had given me a hint, a long time ago, when he said if I knew what a man and woman could do together, I knew what two men could do. Only it wasn't like I imagined at all. Next time I talk to Uncle Sean, I will thank him for not ruining it for me by telling me what two boys could do together! He was right to let me discover it on my own.

I was shaking so bad when Lance and I had undressed, because despite the kissing and hugging we had done, my dream was finally coming true to lay in bed with another boy. Lance knew I was a virgin, and he did make it special. But I think it was special for him too.

I had turned out the lights in the bedroom, but we could still see each other because of the moonlight coming in through the west and north windows. It softened our skin to a glow, and even the bruised side of Lance's face wasn't so harsh and beat up looking. Since it was so hot, we just got under the sheet, and it floated down over us, feather light and kind of cool against our skin.

At first we didn't touch, but we each lay on our backs on our own pillows, and Lance said, "Your sister May was nice to help us do this." In the dark, in the bed, his voice was also soft, but still had that nice, deep resonance I had come to love hearing.

"She surprised me," I told him.

And then we just turned toward each other, and I put my left arm under his neck, and he kind of just rolled into my chest, and then he laid his leg over my side; and when I felt his whole body slide into me and our naked skin came together, it was so wonderfully soft and warm and smooth, without Levi's or under shorts between us, my whole body filled with a kind of heat I'd never felt. When our lips came together in the close embrace, like that, I felt like we were finally connected.

But I had to learn the final thing and, again, I'm glad Uncle Sean did not describe it. Lance had prepared himself in a way I had not noticed, and when he began to move upward a little, where his penis was pressing against my stomach, I was confused, until he took hold of mine and, then, made one last movement. Even now, my eyes fill with tears, and I close them to recall the intensity of the slick warmth he guided me into.

But words fail me, and that's all right. We made love, and he took me the final step into manhood.

Do I love him?

I can't breathe without him! He's my lungs and heart, and my entire being, and I have to live through this day, without him. We came awake in each other's arms just as sunup began to light the room, and we made love again, and if anything, it was even more sweet than the night before. But when we had finished and got up reluctantly, I noticed that he had a troubled look on his face. He put back on his own clothes that May got out of the dryer. Even the blood-stained t-shirt which, more than anything, made him look like the pitiful beat-up kid I had met only two days before on the rock ledge.

"Is there something wrong, Lance? Please tell me that last night was as special for you as it was for me." Even before he answered, I had to fight back tears, because I was afraid—really frightened that Lance was going to tell me that it had been fun, but as always with his 'tricks' it was over. Something anyway, to explain his troubled expression.

In answer, Lance wrapped his arms around me. "It was unbelievably wonderful, Will. Please believe me. I feel like shouting to heaven in thanks for one of its most beautiful angels."

"Then what? You look kind of weird."

He attempted a smile, but it made him just look sad. I noticed that the violet of his eyes turned a little darker, almost brown, when he was troubled or sad, and I intended to take all the darkness from those eyes, if I just had the chance.

"I have to go home, Will."

"Then you're not running away? I thought you couldn't take it anymore!" I heard the hysteria in my voice and I knew it wasn't what he needed, so I took a deep breath, as I did when I was getting a little too emotional before a play on the football field. "I don't understand," I said in a softer voice.

He shook his head. "No. You don't understand. I'm not going home to stay with that son-of-a-bitch! I just need to tell Mom good-bye and thanks for the way she always stood up for me."

I knew he was being sarcastic and bitter, and I hated to hear his rough language after last night. But I bit my tongue and waited for him to continue.

"I also need to let that SOB know I'm walking out of his house for good. I doubt that either of them will care, and I'm glad, now, that I have you." Then he looked at me nakedly, unable to hide the fear in his eyes. "I do, don't I?"

In answer I just hugged him and drew him close and tight. "Don't doubt it for a minute, Lance."

***

Although that was settled between us, I was becoming agitated over breakfast, because I knew Lance was taking a big chance going back home, just so he could tell his mother and stepfather that he was leaving home. I realized, too, that Lance was probably hoping his mother would finally show him the love he craved, and I hurt for him, especially if he found out that she didn't.

I was also afraid he'd be hurt physically. So, I offered to go with him. Even though Daddy was supposed to be operated on this morning and I would be in agony if I wasn't here to find out how it went, I made my decision. I had to be with Lance.

But he refused, and at breakfast, it was just like the morning before. Rita came in and got coffee, and Mrs. Collins brought Trinket back. When Mrs. Collins offered to stay, May and I both told her "no" at the same time, and I think even though she was hurt, she understood.

Then May offered to take Lance home, and when he told her he would appreciate it, I felt hurt. I didn't understand why he didn't want me to go with him. I was an emotional wreck, trying to understand that, and so when Lance and May went out to the pickup, I pulled him aside and told him I didn't understand.

Right there in front of May, he pulled me to him and kissed me on the mouth. "Don't be hurt, Angel! I don't want that SOB to know what you look like. And I don't want to give you a chance of taking him on in a fight. Trust me?"

I couldn't fight the tears that welled up in my eyes, but I tried to make a joke out of it. "Then you should know that May's the one who likes to fight. She'll beat your stepfather to a pulp."

Nobody laughed, though, and I didn't either. I just stood in the drive and watched the pickup disappear down the road. I felt lost and afraid and agitated, but I realized that I had to trust Lance, trust that he did love me as I love him. Of course, it was ridiculously too soon to think in terms of love. But Uncle Sean had said the same thing about him and Theodore Seabrook, and I think my feelings for Lance were at least as genuine as Uncle Sean's feelings for his boyfriend.

Eleven
The Passing

They said Daddy died from internal bleeding. They couldn't pump enough blood into him to keep him alive, and Mama said it was like trying to fill a bathtub without a stopper.

I haven't cried a single tear, not because I'm not sad. It just seemed to happen so fast, and we didn't get a chance to visit with him. The first thing that struck me when Mama called, though she could hardly talk, was *now what am I going to do?* I suddenly feel all the responsibility of the farm resting on my shoulders, and I still have a year of high school left to go. I'm only seventeen years old.

Daddy was only fifty, and this farm got him. I don't want that to happen to me. But now…if I don't stay here and take care of Mama and Rita and Trinket, who's going to? I think May can take care of herself, now that she's graduated and can get a job. So, I don't think I'll have to worry about her.

I've brought the spiral notebook into my room. I suddenly don't care who notices what about my writing. May kind of helped that along when she encouraged me and Lance to have our special night together.

But Daddy. He always said you can make it if you've got hard hands and a strong back, and I have both, and in a way, he had neither, because this farm got him so young. I see ranchers around here that are at least ninety years old, and they seem as strong as mesquite branches and as gnarled, and when I recall Daddy's face, I realize he didn't have many wrinkles, and yet, inside, he must've been a mess, torn up so bad he just bled to death—as Mama said, *like trying to fill a bathtub without a stopper.* I don't think Mama realizes what a horrible image that is—or maybe she does.

Even worse, there won't even be a funeral. Was it something Daddy and Mama had worked out and never discussed with us? It makes me feel like a little kid, again, to just have Daddy go away one day and not have a chance to tell him I loved him! Not have a chance to say I'm sorry for all the times he and I fought!

Mama came home with his ashes in a box this afternoon, and all of us walked out over the farmyard and each took a handful and sprinkled it around; and that was it. We gave him back to the land that took him. She called Julianne and Marsha and told them, and they said they'd be coming home in a few days. She also called her sisters and brothers and, like she said, they were too busy to want to come out here for a funeral, anyway. And Daddy, Mama said, was the youngest in a big old family that was scattered to the four winds years ago when his parents died, which may be why Daddy was like he was: independent, self-made, and not "beholden to nobody" (as he also used to say). We don't even know where his kinfolk are. *None* of them.

It was too hot this afternoon to think deeply about the meaning of us scattering his ashes, out there, where the temperatures are up past a hundred, where the sky is almost as white as the ashes were. I was surprised at their bleached out color, considering that Daddy was dark complexioned, with black hair and dark eyes, and black hair on the backs of his hands.

Mama called Uncle Sean last, because I think they have a closer bond with each other than they do with the rest of Mama's family. So, when she called Uncle Sean, I stayed with her and then talked to him myself. It was good to hear his voice, even under the circumstances, even though he was crying. Like me, he felt guilty for ever having fought with Daddy.

"I'm so sorry I can't come out there, right now," he said. "I hope you understand, Will."

I told him I did and told him Daddy hadn't wanted a funeral, anyway. "Please don't feel bad, Uncle Sean. Mama understands."

"And you, Will? Do you?"

"Of course I do!" I said. "This is a bad time and we just have to get through."

Then I told him a little about Lance, how we met, how we kind of knew right off how much we were drawn to each other. I didn't tell him that we'd already said how much we love each other, but I couldn't keep the joy out of my voice describing him. I'd done so well up to that point while we were talking, until I told him where Lance was, and just as quick as that, my voice broke. "He's gone to tell his parents he's leaving, because of the way they treated him. And I'm scared," I told him. "He's been beat on so much, Uncle Sean! I think I need to take care of him."

Uncle Sean was silent for a little bit, and I was hoping he wouldn't advise me to save myself for the right boy or tell me I was too young to know what I was doing, because Lance is the right boy. So, I waited, fiddling with a pack of cigarettes Mama had left on the counter by the telephone, and her ashtray filled with half-smoked cigarettes.

"You were like that with me," Uncle Sean finally said, and I could hear a kind of break in his voice, too, as if he'd had to take a long, deep breath before he could speak. "But if Lance has any sense," Uncle Sean said, after another moment, "he'll realize what a great boyfriend you'll make."

"Do you think so, Uncle Sean? He's been gone all day."

"I'm sure he's got to work out things at home, Will. It's a big step leaving home, no matter what the reason. Just trust him, okay?"

"Okay," I said. A minute later we said good-bye. As always, I didn't want to stop talking to him, but it was getting on into the afternoon, and I wanted to free up the line in case Lance called.

***

Mama's in her room right now, probably crying privately and, like me, wondering how she's going to take care of us. She says she'll go through Daddy's things for keepsakes, and take his clothes and shoes and whatnot to the church in Hachita—Our Lady of Siena—that was built out of the old high school that shut down here in 1962. Just another sign that

Hachita's dying as quick as trees that aren't watered out here in this desert. But nothing rots, not even the carcass of dead animals. What the buzzards don't eat, the rest turns to leather and then to powder and just blows away.

Trinket cried a lot when she saw her sisters crying about Daddy, and she cried even harder when Mama came back from Deming with the box of ashes, and said Daddy was in there. Trinket said he couldn't be in that little box, because Daddy was so big, but Rita got her aside and said that, no, Daddy wasn't really in that box, and the big part of him was up in heaven looking down on us.

So now I don't have Daddy's advice which, I have to admit, I took less and less in the last couple of years. He wasn't too swift about handing it out, anyway. I think he preferred to see me make my own mistakes; and I sure have. But I loved him. For me he was strong and, when he gave his opinion about stuff that really matters, like treating people with respect, and not saying things you'd be sorry for later, I never failed to understand what he meant—eventually.

He was wrong about Uncle Sean and me, though. Uncle Sean was as honorable as Daddy was.

I can hardly sit still now that the day is closing down. What can be taking so long? I'm trying not to think that he decided he wasn't going to leave home after all. I can NOT think that. I don't want him to be beat on anymore, and I doubt that if he did try to stay at home that the beatings would stop. It's funny, and maybe sad, too, that I can see Lance's face, bruises and all, a lot clearer than I can see Daddy's face.

Maybe it's because I just never looked as closely at Daddy as I did Lance, even though Daddy was there when I was born, and I've seen Daddy almost every day of my life, and now he's gone.

Twelve
Hints of a New Life

Lance came back last night. May and I went and got him. I'm glad she went with me. I think she really likes him and wanted to help.

We were sitting in the kitchen, and everybody was quiet. Mama, because she was probably thinking about Daddy. Rita and Trinket, because they were probably feeling a little lost without Mama being involved with the supper and stuff. May, because of Daddy, and probably the way she and I now shared our new secrets. And I was quiet, because if I had opened my mouth I probably would have begun screaming. All that afternoon, I had thought Lance would call, or show up; but the sun had already set, supper was over, and I was afraid that when he told his stepfather face-to-face that he was leaving, that his stepfather started in beating on him. By then, that's exactly what I thought, and I was crawling the walls with dread.

When the phone rang, everybody jumped. But I flew out of my chair and raced to answer it, and when I heard that soft, deep, oily voice say, "Angel? Can you please come get me?" I began sobbing with relief, and did a bad job of hiding it. So, May came over and took the receiver out of my hand and asked the right questions: where was he, was everything all right, and then she took the pickup keys from me, smiling wanly, and said she was going to drive.

It was a thirty-minute drive up the gravel road from our farm into Hachita, then another fifteen miles west on Highway 9, then another ten miles south, then a few more minutes up to the new town of Playas sitting on the side of the mountain. By the time we got there, it was dark, but May knew right where Lance was. He had called from a pay phone at the Playas town center. He was standing under a street light by the pay phone looking so small and pitiful clutching a small suitcase. He waved when he saw us and before May could pull to a complete stop, I threw the door open and ran across the parking lot like I was going out for a long pass. And when I got close, Lance ran to me and threw himself into my arms. We hugged and kissed right there, and when he cried out in pain, I set him down and looked at his face under the greenish glow of the street light. His lips were big and swollen, and one of his eyes on what had been the good side of his face was black and had swelled up to the size of a golf ball.

"No! Damn that son-of-a-bitch!" I screamed, then growling, "I'll kill him!"

"It's okay! It's okay! It's okay!" he whispered, putting a hand on my chest when he saw how angry I had become.

But I couldn't calm down, and I paced back and forth in the parking lot screaming at the whole town, hating everybody there, as if they were all in on it. And as loud as I was yelling, porch lights began to come on and I even saw the silhouettes of people standing in the glare of the lights looking my way. Then May got out of the pickup and grabbed a handful of my hair, and forced me to look her in the eyes.

"Stop it! Will! Shut up! This town has security guards! You hear me? Let's just get out of here."

I tried to shake her off. "Look what they did to Lance," I said, trying to break out of her grip, but May pulled my hair harder, and I realized that my joke that morning wasn't wrong. She was as strong and capable as I was, and she had me in a hold I couldn't break without going bald, so I held up both hands in surrender. She gave one more yank on my hair and then released me.

A minute later, we were in the pickup, and May drove back down the side of the mountain. Lance was beside me, and I had my left arm around his shoulder; he spoke softly, rubbing my chest. "Angel. Angel. It's okay! I'm out of there, okay?"

I was crying at his new wounds, and felt like a kid. I should have been comforting him, but he was comforting me.

May deliberately drove slowly, while I calmed down. I didn't pay attention to where we were going, whether we were on Highway 9 or near Hachita, or on gravel. And May might as well not have been there, because in a few minutes, Lance and I began kissing and wetting each other's faces with saliva and tears and hugging hard, trying to get closer to each other. I tasted blood in my mouth, from some open wound on Lance's face, but he wouldn't stop devouring me with his mouth, and I couldn't stop, either, until May pulled to a stop at the house.

"Geez! You guys need to cool it just a little," she said, her voice full of laughter and alarm. "You're going to scare Mama to death, Will! Okay?"

So, we did stop, and tried to straighten our clothing. I didn't realize that my face was covered with blood, or that Lance's was, either, until we stepped up on the porch under the light where the moths and other bugs were buzzing around, and I looked at Lance's face which, at the moment, looked like something out of a horror movie. And he looked at me and we both began to laugh and look horrified. So, I ripped off my T-shirt and ran water on it from the hydrant by the oleander bush next to the porch and first washed Lance's face as gently as I could, noting where the blood was coming from. It wasn't as serious as it had looked when he was smeared with blood. Then I scrubbed at my face, until May nodded and took a deep breath. "That'll have to do," she said. She was grinning at me and looking shocked at the same time. "Geez, Will, you're nuts! You know that?"

I knew I was. Uncle Sean had told me how it would be, and it was the truth.

Luckily it was almost ten o'clock when we went into the house. Rita and Trinket were both in bed, and Mama was the only one up.

She looked shocked and angry as soon as she saw that Lance had been beat up again, but she soon calmed down and took him into the bathroom herself and cleaned him up a little better. But when she came back out, saying that Lance was taking a bath, May and I had been talking and decided that we needed to tell Mama what was what. So, she started crying when May and I set her down and told her things about me. It was okay that May didn't mention any of her own secrets. But learning how Lance and I planned to stay together in my room was enough. She objected, saying that Daddy had been right all along, and she wanted to know what Uncle Sean had done to me to turn me "that way," though I was finally able to convince her he had tried to talk me out of my feelings. Of course, I didn't tell Mama that Uncle Sean finally gave in and kissed me, or tell her about the letter he'd written, or that Uncle Sean had a boyfriend, himself, now, and that he and I joked with each other when he called.

She didn't beg me not to have Lance in my room, except maybe with her eyes, nor did she pull rank on me as my mother. But I know that I broke her heart that night, and when I passed by her room and heard her sobbing softly, I figured she was maybe crying even harder for what we told her than she did for Daddy dying.

So, when Lance came out of the bathroom, looking a little cleaner, but with all the new wounds, I knew I simply would not have been able to let him sleep by himself down the hall. He and I put his suitcase into my room and we hung up his clothes. He was looking so nervous and all, asking, "but your mom said this was okay? Don't she know what we'll be doing?"

I was just as nervous as Lance, but I told him it was going to be all right, him and me, sleeping together. I couldn't tell him why it was, but I'd been so scared for him, having gone back to his own parents and facing his father. I couldn't tell him how you had to take things from life, or lose them.

But it's the truth. Maybe Daddy wouldn't understand about Lance, or me being homosexual. But I think he would understand what I've learned from his death and, hopefully, from his life.

I've taken to writing early in the mornings when I wake up and it's cool. Now that I have the notebook in my room, I don't have to sneak out, so that Lance wonders where I am. Though he usually sleeps right through the time I spend writing stuff. My mind is clearer in the mornings, too, and as Mama has said as long as I can remember, things always look different in the morning.

I hope they do for her, too. I hope things look different to her, because another thing I've learned now that Daddy died at so young an age, you have to do things you have to do and not worry how it affects others. The right things, though. I'm not talking about doing mean things, but the right things. Like me and Lance. Seeing how Daddy died so young, I see that it can happen to anybody. So I'm not going to put off being with him at night, just because Mama doesn't like it. So I hope things look different to her in the mornings.

Besides, Lance needs me to heal him from all those years his stepfather hurt him, but even more I'm going to love him and show him that somebody really cares about him, because he needs to heal inside from the wounds his mother inflicted on him — wounds that don't heal so easily. I'm not going to let him suffer a minute longer.

***

Every once in a while, while I'm writing, I look over at him. His face is bruised all over, and the sight in his right eye is a little blurry, but I hope it'll return to normal in a few weeks. I imagine he hurts even while he's sleeping. It hasn't been long enough for the worst of the bruises to heal, and the ones that aren't so bad look a yellow-blue, now, as though someone rubbed eye-shadow on his cheek.

And sometimes, I lay the notebook aside and prop myself up on an elbow and just watch him sleeping. It hurts, he's so beautiful, the way his lids lay over those beautiful eyes, and mask some of the bad things he's seen and been through. When he's sleeping he looks even more like a kid and more innocent.

Then I wake him up by kissing him, and we sometimes make love as the light of day comes into the room, though it's indirect light and just causes his skin to glow. He's the angel, if you want to know the truth.

Mama has been coming along really well with things, since that night we told her everything. But she's like that. She knows that without Lance there with me, I'd have a hard time with the farm work.

May helps out a lot, too.

Trinket has taken up with Lance like she did Uncle Sean. And even though Rita and Mama still lock horns, she and Mama get along better. Don't ask me why or how.

Not only that, but some of the joy I used to feel in the family has returned. Daddy's death is passing into the distance, though we all feel him now and then—especially me, I think, when I'm particularly frustrated working on a piece of equipment. Then I remember how he used to hunch his shoulders, dropping his tools for a minute, then pick them up and go at it again. So that's what I do.

Summer vacation ends in a week and I have one more year of school. Lance and I went in to Animas a few days ago and registered him for school. He'll be a junior, as he lost some time and credits, because of a few bad grades. I don't doubt that he could hardly concentrate on his studies when every night he spent at home was spent in fear of his father. But I'm glad Lance decided he needed to get back in school, even though he's afraid it will be hard. "I know I need a diploma," he said, when he told me he wanted to go back. "I just never thought I could make it through the way things were at home. Maybe with you helping me, I can, Angel."

I've even taken him around to some of my friends to introduce him before school starts. It's such a small school. I didn't want him to feel quite so new on the first day. It'll be neat to have him up in the stands cheering for me when we play football. I'm really tickled at the way Dick Lamb looked when I introduced him the other day. Lance and I were in Hachita for burgers, and I could tell Dick was eyeing Lance as soon as we walked into the Hachita Grill. Of course everybody was eyeing him, because strangers are spotted right off. But Dick was looking awfully hungry when he laid eyes on Lance, so I have no doubt that our great quarterback is exactly as I thought. Who knows, maybe Lance and I can help him find a boyfriend.

The worse thing was going over to Lance's parents' house one Sunday to get his birth certificate and stuff. Mama went with us, and so did May. You'd have never known that the man who answered the door was a monster. He's clean cut-looking, though of course muscled from the kind of work he does. He smiled kind of confused when he saw Lance standing there with me, Mama, and May behind him. But I saw a flicker of something in his eyes that gave him away, as if he would have liked nothing better than to get Lance alone for just a few minutes, though he covered it over by turning and calling to Lance's mother. Nor would you think she was the willing wife of a child-beater. Lance never said, but they're church goers. She was still dressed in what I'd think was her Sunday best and looked about as normal as you can get. I see where Lance gets his violet eyes, and I have to admit that his mother is quite a looker with a lush head of dark-chocolate hair. Lance is just eighteen, and I bet that his mother had him when she wasn't much more than that, herself.

When they invited us all in, we didn't sit or accept the cold drinks Lance's mother offered. It was awkward, but Mama surprised me, and I was proud of her. "No sense in us pretending this is a social call," she said. "We've come to get the rest of Lance's things, including his birth certificate, seeing as how he'll need it to get his life in order."

"And just who the hell do you think you are?" Lance's stepfather asked.

But his wife touched him on the shoulder. "Enough, Richard. This time, just cool it."

I could've filled in the rest of her advice: *Not in front of witnesses, dear.*

Anyway, they have a nice house, and I hope they're happy together now that Lance is living with us. As Lance says in his best sarcasm, they *really deserve* that happiness.

***

Seems like I find less and less time to write, as it has been quite a while since I wrote in this notebook. Lance and I drive to school together every day, and get up early to take care of things, and come home early now that it's just us and May who have to get ready for the harvest. Lance's face is finally clearing up and his beauty continues to startle me. He eats like a horse and is looking more and more solid. And sometimes, when we're out in the field, we just stop and make out for a little bit. The newest thing is his laughter, which just rings through the house sometimes, until everyone just starts laughing along with him. Even Mama, but especially May. She and I catch each other's eyes and smile.

I talked to Uncle Sean, again, the other day, now that Daddy's death isn't so close. I told him how my senior year is going and how Lance is getting along in school, that he has a knack for art, and how he just thrilled the art teacher, Mr. Drummond, to death with renderings he did in charcoal of a few kids in the class. Lance had kept his talent hidden from me this whole two months we've been together, but I heard kids talking about him after school one day and showing off the quick sketches he did of them. So, I told Uncle Sean all about him—and us—and thanked him for not telling me what causes the color in sunsets or what two boys who love each other can do together. Then I said, "Lance sure is pretty, Uncle Sean. He just needs somebody to love him."

"I'm sure you'll take care of that," Uncle Sean said.

—◊—

Editor's Note

That's all there is to the material I found in the barn when I was tearing it down. I hoped that Will Barnett and Lance Surfett made a life for themselves somewhere. How and when the farm near Hachita was abandoned or sold will have to remain a mystery. Too much time has passed and the trail is too cold to follow. And for now it will also have to remain for speculation why Will chose to leave his writing there. Did he intend to return one day and retrieve it? Although he treasured his Uncle Sean's dog tags, he left them in the old barn, too. I find that strange, though I can also attest that nothing in my possession, either, remains from when I was a high school student. Life just intervenes between us and our most precious possessions without our intending it.

***

I finished the project—tearing down the barn and salvaging what I could, storing it for some future use.

But I could not leave the documents alone, and even though possession is nine-tenths of the law, I will always remain a little uneasy about publishing these pages. I did try, however, to pick up that cold, long-time-ago trail.

I visited the old-timers around here, but they just shook their heads when I asked about the Barnett family. No one knew when they'd left. Everyone knew the farm south of Hachita just west of the Big Hatchet Mountain, exactly twenty miles down the paved highway that leads on into Mexico at Antelope Wells.

I had been asked to tear down the old barn by a rancher by the name of Hill, and judging from his age, I figured him to be Old-Man Hill's grandson who Will Barnett talked about. But even he didn't know when the Barnett family left that farm. From what I can figure out about this younger Hill, he must have been a senior in high school before Will entered as a freshman. When I mentioned the name Barnett, the rancher nodded. "Oh yeah, I remember them, all right. There was some strange things that went on there, as I recall. Something about their only boy," he said, "but I can't say exactly what. Some kind of rumors, though. That was a long time ago."

And so it was.

www.ingramcontent.com/pod-product-compliance
Ingram Content Group UK Ltd.
Pitfield, Milton Keynes, MK11 3LW, UK
UKHW041946230426
12048UKWH00008B/156